"I'll play doctor if you'll be my patient,"

Mike teased. His eyes were the green of spring foliage, suggesting secret, shady places perfect for lovers' trysts.

Molly looked at him innocently. "You may be a talented doctor," she said, "but I'm not sick."

"I am." The teasing note was gone from his voice. "I'm sick with wanting you." He moved his fingers up her arm in a slow dance of sensuality that left goose bumps in its wake.

"But the children..." Molly said, breathless from the pleasurable tingles his fingers were creating.

"Yeah, the children," Mike said dryly. "Always the children." There was no rancor in his voice, only weary resignation. He removed his fingers from her arm then, and said, "Molly, come away with me. Don't we owe ourselves just one night...?"

Dear Reader,

The summer is over, it's back to school and time to look forward to the delights of autumn—the changing leaves, the harvest, the special holidays . . . and those frosty nights curled up by the fire with a Silhouette Romance novel.

Silhouette Romance books always reflect the laughter, the tears, the sheer joy of falling in love. And this month is no exception as our heroines find the heroes of their dreams—from the boy next door to the handsome, mysterious stranger.

September continues our WRITTEN IN THE STARS series. Each month in 1991, we're proud to present a book that focuses on the hero—and his astrological sign. September features the strong, enticingly reserved Virgo man in Helen R. Myers's *Through My Eyes*.

I hope you enjoy this month's selection of stories, and in the months to come, watch for Silhouette Romance novels by your all-time favorites including Diana Palmer, Brittany Young, Annette Broadrick and many others.

We love to hear from our readers, and we'd love to hear from *you!*

Happy Reading,

Valerie Susan Hayward
Senior Editor

CARLA CASSIDY

Patchwork Family

Published by Silhouette Books New York

America's Publisher of Contemporary Romance

To Frank, my own true hero, who always believed

SILHOUETTE BOOKS
300 E. 42nd St., New York, N.Y. 10017

PATCHWORK FAMILY

ISBN: 0-373-08818-3

First Silhouette Books printing September 1991

All the characters in this book have no existence
outside the imagination of the author and have
no relation whatsoever to anyone bearing the same
name or names. They are not even distantly
inspired by any individual known or unknown
to the author, and all incidents are pure invention.

®: Trademark used under license and
registered in the United States Patent and
Trademark Office and in other countries.

Printed in the U.S.A.

CARLA CASSIDY

is the author of ten young-adult novels. She's been a cheerleader for the Kansas City Chiefs football team and has traveled the East Coast as a singer and dancer in a band, but the greatest pleasure she's had is in creating romance and happiness for readers.

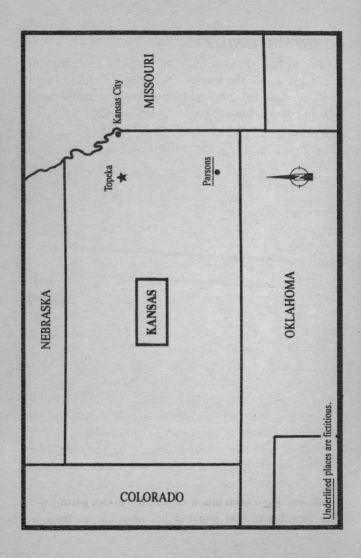

MISSOURI

Kansas City

Topeka ★

Parsons •

NEBRASKA

KANSAS

OKLAHOMA

COLORADO

Underlined places are fictitious.

Chapter One

Dr. Michael Wakefield rolled down his car window, breathing deeply of the cool autumn air. Ah, the smell of the country—somebody could make a fortune if they could bottle it for resale to the weary of the cities of the world. But Mike knew the scent could only be produced by Mother Nature, who knew just the right combination of ingredients—a spoonful of sunshine, a smidgin of rich earth, a pinch of grass and a hint of tang from a nearby cow pasture.

He took another deep breath and shrugged his broad shoulders, trying to work out the kink in the middle of his back. It was a long trip from New York to Parsons, Kansas, especially when the drive was made without stopping except for gas and brief stretches. He'd been much too excited about getting to his new home and starting his new life to turn a twenty-four-hour drive into a thirty-six-hour one complete with motel stop.

A new life. No more Dr. Michael Wakefield, pediatrician to Manhattan's wealthy. From now on it was going to be just plain Mike Wakefield.

For the past eight years, Mike had been baby doctor to the well-to-do of New York City. His patients had longer pedigrees than most Thoroughbreds. But there was one thing he'd learned in those years—well-bred babies with dignified prominent parents had the same manners as any other babies. Mike had been spit up on and burped at, screamed at and kicked. He'd had his eyes poked and his nose pulled, and one rambunctious two-year-old had tried to bite his ear off in a temper tantrum.

After eight years, Mike had come to a startling conclusion: he disliked babies and didn't want to be around them anymore. In fact, he disliked all children under the age of eighteen. But that was all behind him now. He'd made arrangements for his little patients to be cared for by another doctor and was now taking a vacation, something he hadn't done in years. For the next full year he would be leasing a farm in a Kansas town where the average age of the population was sixty-five.

He slowed the car, looking for the gravel-road turnoff that would take him to his new home. He spied the turn and sat up straighter in the seat, anxious for his journey to come to an end.

A smile touched his tired features as he pulled the car off the gravel road and onto a dirt lane lined with heavily laden apple trees. For the next year this was his land. These were his apple trees. It was a far cry from the Fifth Avenue town house he had left behind. His smile widened as he caught a glimpse of the big three-story farmhouse up ahead. He hoped the movers had managed to find the place. What he needed most at the moment was a couple of hours in his favorite recliner chair.

He pulled his car up in front of the large red barn, feeling a euphoric burst of youthful enthusiasm. How many times had he sat in his sterile office, dreaming about living in a place exactly like this?

He threw open his car door and stepped out, twisting slightly to unstiffen his joints. He started to walk toward the house, but then turned and headed for the barn, drawn there by the reality of boyhood fantasies come true. The barn door creaked on rusty hinges as he opened it. He stepped inside, pausing a moment to allow his eyes to adjust to the semidarkness. He breathed deeply, savoring the scents of rubbed leather, old hay and the underlying musk of horses no longer there.

"My workshop," he murmured aloud, easily imagining the interior of the barn as the woodworking shop he'd always dreamed of having. The owner had already given permission for him to do whatever he wanted to make the place comfortable.

He frowned as his gaze swung to one corner of the barn where a strange design appeared to have been spray-painted on the wall. Orange crates were overturned to make chairs, and a squat candle, half-burned, sat ready for use. "What's all this?" he asked aloud. Somebody had been using his barn. He'd read about things like this, strange cults using abandoned buildings for their bizarre rituals. He spied a paper cup on the floor and picked it up. It was filled with a purple liquid. He sniffed it and frowned in confusion. He'd never read about a cult who had a penchant for grape juice.

He was suddenly filled with the same outrage he'd felt two months ago when he'd been robbed by a pickpocket. He felt violated and angry. Somebody had been using his barn for who knew what purpose. He studied the picture sprayed on the wall. It looked sort of like an ear.

He whirled around as he heard the side door creak open. Two boys walked in, stopping short at the sight of him. They were about twelve. One was red-haired and one dark, and they both looked guilty as hell. Eyes widening, they turned on their heels and took off at a run.

"Hey, wait a minute!" he yelled. "I want to talk to you boys." They had walked into the barn with a proprietary air, and he had a feeling that, if he wanted to get some answers about who was using the barn, he needed to catch those kids. Without another thought, he took off in pursuit, running out of the barn and across a field.

As Mike raced after the two boys, he soon realized he was functioning with several disadvantages. First and foremost, he was thirty-four years old and the last time he'd run he'd been after a four-year-old who had gotten hold of his stethoscope and taken off down the office hallway with the speed of the cartoon coyote. The Italian shoes Mike was now wearing were made to look good, but they weren't exactly great track-and-field equipment.

"Ouch!" he cried breathlessly as his foot hit a rut, causing one of the expensive shoes to fly off into the air behind him. He didn't slow his pace, knowing he could pick up the shoe on the trip back. As he continued to run, his chest heaving and sweat breaking out on his forehead, he knew one of two things was going to happen: either the boys would wear down and stop and he would catch them, or he would drop dead. He was beginning to fear the latter.

He grunted in triumph as he saw the neighboring farmhouse come into view and realized that was where the culprits were headed. Good, at least he could have a talk with the boys' father, find out what nefarious use his barn had fulfilled.

By the time Mike reached the front yard of the house, the boys had disappeared, but he hardly noticed. He gave only a moment's attention to the house, which although small, was meticulously neat, with the remnants of a flower garden across the front and a sweeping porch that held a wooden rocking chair and a swing. What Mike did notice was a young girl standing in the center of a flock of chickens, carefully scattering feed to the squawking pecking creatures. Another young girl was swinging in a tire swing that hung from a huge oak tree by the side of the house. These two looked to be about the same age as the boys he'd chased out of the barn and he wondered if the four were quadruplets. The women in Kansas must be as fertile as the soil, he thought, startled as he felt a tug on the leg of his slacks. He looked down into the bright blue eyes of child number five, a blond-haired moppet of about five who was sitting by the edge of a puddle of mud.

"Hi, I'm making pies." She smiled, exposing a missing front tooth.

"So I see," Mike answered, stepping back from her and stifling a groan as he saw the perfect muddy handprint that marred the beige of his slacks.

At that moment, the front door opened and a young woman stepped out onto the front porch. "Supper's ready," she called, her voice low and rich as a cup of hot coffee on a cold wintry morning. Immediately the kids clamored for the porch, creating enough noise to make Mike aware of the beginning of a whopper of a headache.

"I made pies for dessert," the little girl next to Mike yelled toward the house, and it was then that the woman saw him.

She immediately left the front porch, moving with a graceful ease Mike might have admired had he not been so disgruntled.

What he did notice was that her shoulder-length hair was the color of ripe wheat and the jeans and sweat-shirt she wore did nothing to hide her lush curves. Her face still held the vestiges of a summer tan, which only emphasized the amused sparkle of her blue eyes and the small upward curve of her lips.

"When I want to feel the Kansas dirt beneath my feet, I usually take off both shoes and my socks," she said, smiling with friendly humor, her eyes dancing down his body and lingering in amusement at his shoeless foot.

Her words made him realize how ridiculous he probably looked. His chest was still heaving with exertion, and his shirt was damp with perspiration. His slacks were decorated with a muddy handprint, and one foot was shoeless. Mike was a man who prided himself on his dignified appearance. He'd long ago perfected the art of emitting an aura of calm while some colicky baby threw up on him. He called on that inner resource now, squaring his broad shoulders and facing her solemnly. "Are those your children?" He made no indication that he'd appreciated her attempt at levity. Instead he pointed stiffly to the children gathered on the front porch.

"Every last one of them, including this muddy mess." Her voice was full of pride as she leaned down and swooped up the pint-size pie-maker, unmindful of the little girl's mud-caked hands.

"Well, I caught two of them trespassing in my barn," He eyed the girls on the porch. "Two boys— one of them was red-haired and freckled and the other one was dark-haired."

"Oh, you must be our new neighbor." She smiled fully up at him. "You bought the Wiley place?"

"I've leased it. Now, about your boys—"

She nodded. "The red-haired one is Scotty, and the other one is Jimmy." She turned back to the girls on the porch. "Carrie, go find Scotty and Jimmy. They're probably in their room."

One of the two older girls nodded and took off into the house. She reappeared seconds later flanked by the guilty culprits.

Mike was surprised to see the woman using sign language with the two boys, who quickly signed back to her. No wonder they hadn't stopped when Mike had called to them. They hadn't been able to hear. She watched the boys' flying fingers for a moment, then laughed and signed back, this time making the two boys giggle.

The thread of patience Mike had been holding on to snapped. He'd been greeted at his new home by juvenile members of some strange cult, he was tired and cranky, and the last straw was this woman with her miniature mobsters laughing at him.

"I certainly hope they aren't telling you they weren't in my barn," he snapped.

"Oh, no, they plead guilty," she said, laughing. "But they said you frightened them. They thought you were a monster of some kind."

"Well, in the future I would appreciate it if you would keep your children out of my barn," Mike said. And out of my life, he added mentally.

The pleasant smile on her face vanished as quickly as the sun skirting behind a gray cloud. "No problem. I'll make sure the kids don't trespass again." Gone was all trace of her former warmth and good humor.

"How many kids are there, anyway?"

"Five, and one on the way," she replied.

"Why aren't they in school?"

"There was a teachers' meeting." She eyed him defiantly, letting him know it really wasn't any of his business.

He nodded wearily. The effects of his long trip hit him all at once, making him numb with fatigue. "Thank you for your time. I appreciate your understanding."

"Oh, I think we understand each other perfectly," she said, her blue eyes decidedly cool. "Now, if you'll excuse me, I have five hungry children waiting for dinner."

Mike watched as she walked to the front porch, then disappeared into the house.

He turned and slowly began the trek back across the field to where he had lost his shoe. Five kids—the woman and her husband were either saints or lunatics. Still, he wondered what was wrong with the two boys' hearing. Was it genetic, a birth defect, or had their deafness been caused by some sort of accident? Mike shoved his doctoring instincts aside as he stepped into his errant shoe. Kids—who needed them? He looked down at his mud-stained slacks and grimaced, then made his way toward his new home.

It was just his dumb luck. He'd taken a year off, moved halfway across the country to escape having kids in his life, and what had he done? Moved right next door to the "woman who lived in a shoe." What else could possibly go wrong?

*   *   *

Molly Smith leaned back in the rocking chair on the front porch, pulling her sweater closer around her neck against the chill night air. Funny, it seemed she spent all day long waiting and wishing for the kids' bedtime to arrive, longing for when the house would be quiet and she could have time for herself. But always, when this hour of the day finally came, she found the house too quiet—lonely. Still, this was the first opportunity she'd had to think about her new neighbor.

Supper in the Smith household was certainly not the time to attempt any sort of thought at all. Supper was accomplished through a combination of effective efficiency, team cooperation and controlled chaos.

Following supper was bathtime, another study in patience and cooperation. Finally came bedtime, and the house took on a quiet that was unnatural.

Molly leaned her head back and looked up at the stars, thinking of the man who'd leased the Wiley farm. He'd certainly been a looker, with his thick dark hair just beginning to go gray at the temples and those drop-dead gorgeous eyes. Sort of a mixture of gray and green, like the green dress she'd bought two years earlier and had never been able to find a pair of shoes to match.

She'd known in an instant that he wasn't from around here. No store in town sold the kind of tailored silk shirt that had hugged his broad shoulders, tapering perfectly to his slender waist. Her first instinct had been proved right when he had spoken, his voice a low deep rumble with an East Coast accent. He was obviously very... cosmopolitan, and it had been equally obvious that he didn't like kids. She smiled as she thought of Maggie's muddy handprint on his pant leg. Served him right, she thought defiantly, taking a sip from her mug of coffee. He hadn't even asked why the kids were in the barn. He'd just stiffly demanded they stay out.

Oh, she knew his type. A preppie who was devoted to his career. His wife was probably a willowy red-head who refused to sacrifice her reed-thin figure for the experience of giving birth.

Molly didn't have to worry about losing a reed-thin figure. The last time she'd been considered willowy was when she was twelve, with scabby knees and dirty elbows. But then, Molly had never experienced the joy of birth, either. As a foster parent and the neighbor-hood baby-sitter, she got all the pleasures of mother-ing without the actual birth experience. Maybe someday she would have the pleasure of both. But for now, each little person who stayed in her home, each broken and lonely child the agency sent her, became one of her own, and when they eventually left, they always took a part of Molly's heart with them. Even the kids for whom she baby-sat held a special place deep within her. She smiled, realizing she should have told her new neighbor that the kids weren't really all hers. At the moment she had three foster children; the other two were the kids she watched during the day. But he had looked so outraged, so disgruntled by the number of children, she'd just automatically called them all her own.

"He must be a very unhappy man," she murmured aloud. To her mind, any person who didn't like children either didn't know anything about them, or had a basic character flaw. Molly found herself wondering which applied to her neighbor.

"Enough of this," she said, draining her coffee cup and standing up. The kids would be up early tomorrow—they always were—and she was exhausted. Besides, she'd wasted enough of her time thinking about a man who had been a stiff self-righteous prig. She should be spending her time thinking about how she was going to come up with enough money for the room addition she desperately needed. With this new worry in mind, Molly headed for bed.

"Tomorrow or the next day?" Mike yelled into the phone receiver. "Look, I paid you a small fortune to see that my things would be here before I arrived." He slammed down the receiver in frustration.

Terrific, the moving van with all his furniture had engine trouble and was stuck in some po-dunk town in Indiana.

"Somebody's put a curse on me," he muttered. It was the only explanation for the run of bad luck that had plagued him from the moment he had spied the boys in his barn.

He'd spent a miserable night on the floor, huddled beneath a blanket he'd thrown into the trunk of his car before beginning his cross-country trip. When he'd awakened, he realized the kink in his back had mated with the one in his shoulder, and reproduction had taken place, resulting in little baby kinks all over his body.

He jumped in surprise as the phone rang. It had better not be the moving company with another problem, he thought, grabbing up the receiver. "Hello," he growled.

"My, my, my, it certainly doesn't sound like all that country air is improving your temperment."

Mike relaxed as he recognized the smooth feminine voice. "Hello, Celia. Let's just say at the moment I'm finding country life rather stressful."

"Poor darling. Tell Celia all about it."

Mike grinned, knowing she would revel in every complaint he voiced. Celia Warren had been Mike's favorite female companion and a good friend for the past three years. She had also been one of the loudest protesters when he had announced his decision to spend a year in Kansas.

"Tell me, darling. I want to hear every dreadful detail. You've left me up here escortless, having to relegate myself to having Wally the worm for a date, so I think it only fair that you should be utterly miserable."

Mike laughed. "Now, Celia, Wally's not such a bad guy."

"He's not a bad guy—for a worm," she replied. "And if I date him long enough maybe he'll give me a face-lift gratis."

"It will be a very long time before you have to concern yourself about any cosmetic surgery," Mike replied with a small smile, knowing how Celia thrived on compliments.

"Oh, darling, I do miss you." She laughed. "Now seriously, tell me how things are going."

Mike sighed. "Okay, I guess. My furniture is stuck someplace in Indiana. The electricity hasn't been turned on yet, and my nearest neighbor belongs in the Guinness Book of Records for most prolific breeder."

"Wonderful. So why don't you just forget all this nonsense and move back to civilization where you belong?"

Mike laughed again. "Oh, no, I'm not giving up this easily. I'm from pioneer stock. My forefathers crossed the prairie in a covered wagon. Surely I can put up with a little inconvenience for a couple of days."

"Mike, honey. You can't fool me. The only prairie your forefathers crossed was driving from Long Island into Manhattan in a Lincoln Town Car." She smoothly overrode Mike's laughing protest. "I think this 'back to the earth' mind-set of yours is nothing more than a midlife crisis. You should have just waited for it to pass and spent your weekends at the club. If you wanted green grass and fresh air, the golf course would have sufficed."

Mike started to explain to her that it hadn't been just a need for air and sunshine, that it had been something much more, but he knew without a doubt that no matter what he said, Celia would never understand. Celia's idea of a picnic was lunch at the Plaza in a seat next to the window. Her idea of a day in the country was a buggy ride through Central Park. No, Celia was strictly a city girl. And Mike, well, he wasn't sure exactly what he was. He only knew this move had fed some need in him.

"So, when are you coming back for a visit?" Celia asked, and Mike could tell by her tone of voice that her lips were formed into her famous pout.

"Celia, I've only been gone for two days."

"I know, but it already seems like forever. Maybe I'll surprise you and come out there for a visit."

"You know you'd be welcome," he replied.

"Well, I'd better run. I've got an appointment with Harry at ten. We're going to delve into what happened in my childhood that makes me crave cheesecake as an adult."

"Now, that's going to take some serious psychoanalysis." Mike laughed, realizing the conversation with Celia had effectively managed to banish the ill humor with which he'd awakened.

"Ciao, darling, I'll keep in touch." There was a click, signaling she had hung up.

With a smile still lingering on his lips, Mike replaced the receiver, then crossed to the kitchen window and looked outside. "What a view," he murmured in appreciation. No buses, no people, nothing but Mother Nature at her best. Even though it was just a few minutes before eight o'clock, already the sun was shining through the window and dancing through the autumn-colored leaves of the trees, promising a warm fall day.

Fishing—the day was going to be perfect for it. Mike smiled to himself in boyish anticipation at the thought of the large pond the owner had promised was stocked full of catfish and crappie. Luckily he'd bought a brand-new rod and reel and a tackle box full of the latest lures before he'd left New York. All he had to do was pull the new equipment out of the trunk, go down to the pond, and voilà—lunch. But first, what he needed more than anything was a hot shower to wash away the soreness of his muscles. He headed for the bathroom, thinking about the stringer full of fish he'd have by noon. He'd barbecue them over the old brick pit in the backyard. There was something infinitely appealing about the primitive notion of catching his meal and cooking it over an open fire. Maybe there was a Daniel Boone in his ancestral tree. In any case, he was already feeling the first pangs of hunger, so by noon he'd be ravenous.

He went into the bathroom and instantly felt his foul mood rushing back to claim him. When the Wileys had shown him the house, he'd instantly fallen in love with the beauty of the wooded area, the spaciousness of the big house and the charm of the stone fireplace. What Mike hadn't noticed was the antiquated plumbing in the bathroom. Shower, hell. He'd be lucky to get a teacupful of hot water out of the rusty old faucets above the tub. And speaking of tubs, this one was unusually deep and short, standing on four clawed feet that looked as if they belonged on the bottom of a pair of eagles.

Pioneer stock, he reminded himself grimly, turning on the faucets, which squealed in protest at each revolution. Rusty water spewed out. "Yuck," he muttered eloquently, borrowing one of his former patient's favorite words. He watched the water, sighing with relief as it cleared and—glory be—began to steam. The sight made him laugh out loud. He had a feeling that a cold bath might have been the last straw that would have sent him packing and heading back to civilization, as Celia put it.

He plugged the drain, then quickly stripped off his clothes and climbed in, folding his six-foot-plus length like a contortionist trying to get into a small suitcase.

A hiss of pleasure escaped his lips as he found a bearable position and leaned his head back, allowing the deep tub to continue to fill.

"Just what the doctor ordered," he mumbled, shutting off the water that now lapped around his shoulders. His position was less than dignified, but the bath was serving his purpose, the heat of the water making his muscles relax and unkink.

The first thing he had to do was install a shower. The tub really wasn't too bad, but he didn't want to make it an everyday thing. He'd also noticed that the railing on the steps leading up to his front porch was wobbly and needed to be fixed. He began making a mental list of chores. Chores—that had a nice country ring to it. No appointments to keep, no patients waiting, no anxious mothers to soothe, just good old-fashioned chores. And that was something he could handle. He'd worked as a carpenter's helper for a couple of summers to help pay his way through medical school. It would be good to get back to some physical work, keep his mind off his New York practice and the pain of failure.

"Nothing like a nice hot bath and a plan of action to make the world right with a man," he said aloud. Okay, so things had gotten off to a rocky start. From here on it was going to be smooth sailing.

He sank lower in the tub, immersing his head beneath the water, then coming up sputtering with sheer pleasure. He had just come up for the third time when he realized somebody was knocking on his door.

He got out of the tub reluctantly and grabbed a towel, then jerked on a clean pair of slacks and hurried to the door. He yanked it open and took a step onto the porch. "What the hell?" he gasped, then looked down to see his foot planted squarely in the center of an apple pie.

Chapter Two

Molly had just walked down the steps of the porch when she heard the door open. Before she had a chance to utter a warning, his foot landed right in the middle of the pie.

Other than his initial expletive, he didn't say a word, merely glared at her as if she had purposely placed the pie where he'd step on it.

"Well, I've heard of the old pie-in-the-face trick," Molly said. "Is this a new variation?" Molly hoped her sense of humor, which had helped her survive both big and small tragedies in the past, would come to her aid now. She held her breath, waiting for his response, wondering if her attempt to lighten the situation would be met kindly or if she'd receive the same cool disdain she'd met the previous day. She'd fought with herself over whether to bring the pie to him at all.

Finally, deciding she'd rather be on friendly terms with a new neighbor than unfriendly, she decided to make an extra effort.

"It's such a shame," he said slowly, looking down at his pie-covered toes. "It feels like you cooked the apples to just the right consistency—soft, but not mushy, crisp, but not hard." He wiggled his toes, then looked back up at her and offered a small smile.

Laughter bubbled up in her, releasing itself in a combination of giggles and apology. "I'm really sorry. I thought you might enjoy an apple pie, sort of a welcome to the area. I knocked several times and when you didn't answer, I thought I'd just leave it for you."

"I was taking a bath," he replied, looking down once again at the mess on his foot. "Uh, could you do me a favor?"

She nodded, for a moment unable to speak as she suddenly realized how attractive, how utterly male, he looked. She'd been too concerned about his anger to notice before. His hair was damp and tousled, stealing the dignified air he'd worn like a shield the day before. He was shirtless, exposing a firmly muscled chest sprinkled with thick wavy hair.

"I dropped a towel in the bathroom. Could you grab it for me? I'd hate to trail this mess through the house."

"Towel?" She looked at him blankly for a moment, then mentally shook herself, a warm blush sweeping over her. "Sure," she mumbled, moving up the three steps of the porch, then around him and into the house.

Did I think he was a looker yesterday? she mused as she walked through the large empty living room and headed for the staircase that led upstairs to the bathroom and three bedrooms. I was wrong. He's positively gorgeous, she mentally amended.

She had no trouble finding the bathroom—she knew exactly where to go. She'd visited the Wileys often when they had lived here, and she'd always loved this house. It was three times the size of hers and would have been perfect for raising her ever growing brood. Unfortunately, the rent was about three times what she could afford. Still, as she made her way to the bathroom, she couldn't help but admire the rich oak woodwork, the spaciousness of the rooms. She went into the bathroom, where she immediately spied the thick navy towel hanging on the towel rack. She grabbed it, then hurried back downstairs and outside, where she found him sitting on the first step.

She handed him the towel, then sat beside him. "I like your furniture. I've always appreciated unobtrusive decor." She grinned.

"Not amusing," he answered, but his eyes sparkled more green than gray, lit with a touch of a smile that didn't quite curve his lips. "The moving truck broke down on the way, so all my furniture is stuck someplace by the side of the road."

"I've got a whole barnful of old furniture. It's nothing great, but I'd be more than happy to loan you some things until yours arrive." She smiled as he looked at her in surprise. "It's obvious you aren't from around here."

He shook his head. "No, I'm from New York, and there nobody offers you a loan of anything, and if they want something you have, they just take it."

She nodded. "I visited New York for a couple of days about ten years ago. For some people, it's like an elixir—the fast pace, the people, the commotion—but to me it was utter horror." She smiled at him and held out her hand. "By the way, I'm Molly Smith."

"Michael Wakefield." He took the hand she held out.

"It's obvious you aren't an experienced farmer," she said, holding his hand for just a moment.

"Why?" He looked affronted.

"Your hands are a dead giveaway." Molly released his.

"What's wrong with them?" he demanded, his eyes graying slightly.

Molly laughed. "Nothing is wrong with them, but they're soft, manicured—the hands of a gentleman, not a farmer."

He studied his palms, as if he'd never really looked at them before. He smiled ruefully. "I bought everything I thought I would need to begin a life as a farmer. The only thing I couldn't find in any of the stores was a pair of thickly callused hands."

"Don't worry, time and work provides those." She was pleasantly surprised to discover that she was enjoying him, that beneath his staid exterior lurked a sense of humor. "Is your wife going to be joining you later?"

"I'm not married."

"Oh." Molly slowly digested this new bit of information. Not only gorgeous, but unattached. She had been hoping for a nice young couple with a few kids as her new neighbors, but she certainly wasn't disappointed in the prospect of an attractive bachelor living right next door to her. "So, what did you do back in the Big Apple?" she asked curiously.

"I was a doctor." A strange expression came over his face as he focused his attention on cleaning off his foot with the towel.

Molly waited for him to elaborate, but he didn't. "Well," she said, "the offer of the furniture still stands."

"That's really nice of you, but I'm hoping mine will turn up sometime today." He wiped the last of the apple off his foot. He looked at her and smiled, a warm smile that turned his eyes a sea-green and made a dimple appear in his cheek. "Still, I really appreciate the offer. And I haven't thanked you for the pie and the bread." He gestured to the loaf that sat next to the ruined pie.

"Oh, it's no big deal," she replied, almost breathless at his attractiveness. "I believe in being neighborly." She stood up. "I guess I'd better get back to the house. It's usually dangerous to leave the kids at home alone for very long." She noticed the way his eyes instantly grayed at the mention of the children.

"I can just imagine the damage five kids can do when left unattended." Again, Molly heard the cool disdain in his voice, and the interest she'd felt toward him waned, replaced by a tinge of disappointment.

"Actually, they're a pretty good bunch."

"I'm sure," he answered in a tone that was rife with condescension.

Molly opened her mouth to protest, then firmly snapped it shut. She'd be damned if she was going to defend her kids to anyone, especially him.

But there was one thing she wanted him to know. "About the boys using your barn—Mr. Wiley let them use it as a clubhouse. They didn't realize you had moved in, and so didn't realize they were trespassing. I'll see to it that they understand."

"Thank you. It was nice meeting you, Molly." He smiled, but the warmth was gone.

"Same to you," she answered, then turned and began the walk back to her house.

Why was it all the men in the world who were single and attractive didn't like kids? she wondered. Why was it that only men like Mister Rogers enjoyed the pleasures of having little people around? Mister Rogers was fine in small doses, but it was difficult to imagine a wild passionate love affair with him. Of course at this point in her life it was difficult to imagine a wild passionate affair with anyone. She'd come close with David—close, but no cigar.

Her footsteps slowed as she thought of David Jackson, the fiancé who'd never made it to the altar. She'd met him two years ago at a community-center dance and they had instantly hit it off. He was an insurance salesman and owned a large house in town, and Molly had been drawn to his good sense of humor and stability. At forty-seven, David was financially secure and emitted an aura of contentment with his life. There had been no crazy sparks between them, just a warmth and respect that had made them comfortable companions. When David had asked her to marry him, she hadn't hesitated in accepting. It wasn't until a month before the wedding that Molly realized there were a couple of things she'd failed to learn about David, such as the fact that he'd just assumed she would no longer be a foster parent once they were married.

David had presented her with a choice: marriage to him or her kids. It had really been no choice at all. She loved David, but the kids were her very life. It wasn't until later, when the engagement was only a memory, that Molly came to the realization that had David loved her enough, he would have never forced her to choose between him and the children. He would have known that marriage to her was a package deal.

"Love me, love my kids," she muttered, carefully picking her way over the ruts in the field that separated her house from the Wiley place. She knew this attitude was rather rigid, but she could have it no other way. She had enough memories of her own childhood to remember what it felt like not to be wanted. She'd make certain the man in her life would never make her kids feel that way.

"Michael Wakefield." She rolled his name off the tip of her tongue, experiencing a small feeling of regret. It was obvious he didn't like kids, and that was a real shame. When he had smiled at her, causing his dimple to dance in his cheek, she'd felt a spark that had begun in her toes and hit her heart like a flame, making her warm from the inside out.

"Huh, probably a premature hot flash," she scoffed as her house came into view. Yes, it was really too bad, but any man who didn't like kids certainly didn't have a place in her life.

Mike watched her go, admiring the way the morning sun sparkled on her hair, like light playing on the surface of a prism. And the scent of her... When she had sat down next to him on the stoop he'd been distracted by her scent, a mixture of cinnamon, apples and freshly baked bread. The woman had smelled positively edible.

He picked up the ruined pie and the loaf of bread and went into the house. Molly—the name somehow fit her. A Midwest sort of name for a Midwest sort of farm woman. A very married farm woman, he reminded himself. Five children and one on the way— how much more married could you get than that? With a professional detachment, he considered her condition. Physically, there certainly wasn't any indication of her pregnancy. Granted, she wasn't model thin, not like Celia who managed to keep a rapier-thin figure by feasting on cheesecake one day and fruit juice and lettuce leaves the next. No, Molly was all shapely curves that promised a man endless possibilities.

Married curves, Mike reminded himself, pulling on a clean shirt. He thought about his curtness when she had asked him what he'd done back in New York.

Lord, imagine what his life would be like if she discovered he was a pediatrician!

Enough time wasted thinking about her, Mike chided himself. If she could keep her kids on their own side of the fence, then she'd make a very pleasant neighbor and nothing more.

Almost a half hour later he made his way down the lane behind the house that led to the large pond. He was carrying his new fishing pole, the tackle box full of the latest lures and a cooler full of beer. The sun was warm on his back and a whistle found its way to his lips as he felt months and months of stress falling away from him like an old skin ready to be shed.

Ah, this was what he'd dreamed about when he had been in his Manhattan office handing out vaccinations and lollipops with the same efficiency.

He'd needed a vacation, time out to reassess the priorities in his life. He'd been so successful so quickly in his practice, thought he had the world on a string, until things fell apart a month ago. He shoved these thoughts away, still finding them too painful to deal with. He didn't want to think about work. He only wanted to enjoy the solitary sport of catching fish.

He found a comfortable spot next to the pond and sat down, taking a moment to enjoy the beauty of his surroundings. The pond was located in a clearing, and around it were thick groves of trees, all displaying vivid autumn dress. The grass that covered the ground of the clearing was still soft and green as if yet unaware of winter's steady approach. But, what impressed Mike most was the silence. Other than the whisper of a breeze rustling the drying leaves of the nearby trees, there was an almost reverent hush.

With a satisfied sigh, he opened his tackle box and stared in dismay. So many colors, so many shapes and sizes—how was he supposed to know which lure would catch a fish? The salesman in the sporting-goods store had talked about water temperature and pH measurements, but Mike hadn't really paid much attention. He reached blindly into the box and grabbed a bright yellow lure that looked like a miniature version of a child's nightmare monster bug. He tied it on his line and cast into the water. Then, popping the top of a can of beer, he settled back to wait for lunch.

He wasn't even aware he'd fallen asleep until a sound jerked him back to consciousness. What was it? The noise seemed to be coming from the grove of trees on the opposite side of the pond—music and laughter breaking the reverent silence he'd enjoyed earlier. The noise had the same effect of a marching band suddenly parading through the middle of a church service.

His eyes narrowed as Molly and her brood broke into the clearing, complete with boom box, picnic basket and fishing poles.

"Oh, no, not at my pond, you don't," he muttered irritably. "What are you doing here?" he yelled across the pond, trying to keep the irritation out of his voice. He realized he'd failed when he saw her shoulders stiffen.

"What does it look like we're doing?" she answered, gesturing at the kids who were scattered around her side of the pond, poles dangling over the water.

Mike bit the inside of his cheek in abject annoyance. Perhaps a compromise was in order. "I don't mind if you want to fish my pond, but couldn't you do it after I'm finished?"

"How kind of you to offer us access to your pond." Her voice was excruciatingly polite. "However, if you study your land survey, you'll discover that this half of the pond is on my property."

Mike wanted to insist that she take her noisy offspring and vacate the premises, but he vaguely remembered the Wileys' mentioning something about boundary lines and the pond, and he had a sinking suspicion that Molly was correct. "Could you at least see to it that the kids are quiet so they don't spook the fish?" he asked tightly.

"I'll do my best, but you know how unruly children can be." Mockery was thick in her voice, and as if to prove her point one of the boys turned up the volume on the radio.

Terrific, Mike scowled. How was he supposed to catch fish with the kids' noisy voices filling the clearing and rock-and-roll music blaring obscenely. His impulse was to leave, come back later when his peace and quiet wouldn't be disturbed. But his stubborn nature refused to allow him to be bullied away from his half of the pond by a blond farm matron and her youthful marauders.

He glared in irritation as one of the boys suddenly whooped with excitement and began frantically reeling in his line. At the other end was a fish worth mounting.

Mike's annoyance continued to climb as first one child then another pulled in fish, and with each catch the others whooped and hollered encouragement.

"How are they doing it?" Mike grumbled, staring accusingly at his own line. He hadn't had a bite, not one single nibble. To add to his indignity, his stomach rumbled loudly in hunger. He reeled in his line and changed the lure, choosing a fluorescent green bug with bulging silver eyes. He threw his line into the water and once again directed his glare back across the pond to where Molly was showing one of the boys how to cast.

Despite his exasperation he couldn't help but admire Molly's attractiveness. He'd noticed earlier in the day that she had the glowing complexion that came from a healthy diet and plenty of exercise. She'd hadn't been wearing makeup when she'd brought him the pie. Of course, it had been early in the morning, but Mike had a feeling that Molly was the type of woman who didn't take time for such things as makeup. With five kids, how could she take time for herself?

He felt a tingle of pleasure ripple through him as she raised a pole over her head to cast, the action causing her T-shirt to ride up, exposing a firm smoothly tanned stomach.

"Are you Scrooge?"

Mike jumped at the sound of the childish voice coming from behind him. He turned to see the mud-pie maker from the previous day, a thumb anchored securely in her mouth while her blue eyes studied him soberly. "I beg your pardon?"

"We saw a movie once about a grouchy old man who tried to ruin Christmas. Are you Scrooge?"

It was amazing how clearly the little girl was able to enunciate around the obstacle of her thumb. "No, I'm not Scrooge. I'm just a grouchy old man," Mike replied. He turned back around to watch his line.

The little girl moved next to him, close enough for Mike to smell the scent that only youth could produce. It was not an unpleasant odor—a touch of sweat, a bit of sunshine and the overriding sweetness of innocence. At the moment, it was unpleasant only because of the emotions it evoked, reminding him of all he'd left behind.

"How come?"

"How come what?" He looked into clear blue eyes that studied him curiously, as if he were an alien from another planet.

"How come you're grouchy?"

Why is this happening to me? What sin have I committed in the past that I'm now being punished for? Mike wondered dismally. "I'm grouchy because I don't like little girls talking to me while I'm catching fish."

"But you aren't catching fish," she said with an honesty that made Mike wince.

"That's because you're talking and scaring all the fish away."

A smile appeared on either side of her thumb. "Fish don't have ears, silly grouch."

Mike flushed. Just what he needed, a lesson on the anatomy of fish from a five-year-old. "What flavor is your thumb?" he asked gruffly, wishing Molly would look over and see the child bothering him.

"Worm flavor." It came out "worm flabor" due to the intrusion of her thumb. Still, Mike wasn't sure he'd heard correctly.

"What flavor?" he repeated.

"Worm." She reached into her pocket and withdrew several slightly smooshed, still-squirming earthworms. "We dug 'em up before we came fishing."

"Is that what everyone is using for bait?" She nodded, and Mike thought about all the fish they had been pulling from the pond. He'd spent a small fortune in lures and all he needed was a couple of worms. He smiled at the little girl. "Would you give me a couple of your worms?"

The blue eyes studied him for a long moment. "Nah, my worms don't like grouches." With this pronouncement she shoved the worms back in her pocket, then turned and went skipping off to her own side of the pond.

I hate kids, Mike thought mournfully as his stomach rumbled an eight on the Richter scale. *I didn't want fish for lunch, anyway,* he rationalized, reeling in his line and putting the unsuccessful lure back in the tackle box. *I'll just drive into town and eat lunch at one of the cafés. I need to buy some things, anyway.* He looked across the pond, where the kids had abandoned their poles and were giggling and dancing to the beat of the music. Molly was sitting next to the radio, the two deaf boys on either side of her. Their fingers were flying as they communicated back and forth. Occasionally the boys would place their hands on top of the radio speaker, feeling the vibrations of the pounding music. Once again Mike found himself wondering about the cause of their deafness.

"I'm not a pediatrician anymore," he muttered, standing up and grabbing his cooler, tackle box and pole. So much for his quiet peaceful morning of fishing. He turned to leave, but was stopped by a childish squeal of pain. He turned to see the little girl running toward Molly, her eyes wide with tears and incoherent yelps coming from her mouth.

"Is she all right?" Mike yelled, setting down his things.

"She's got a hook in her finger." Molly leaned down and spoke soothingly to the near-hysterical little girl. "Don't worry about it, we'll be fine," Molly yelled back at him, defiant independence in her voice.

With a sigh of resignation, Mike strode to the other side of the pond where all the kids were gathered around Molly and the weeping child.

"I said we'll be fine," Molly protested. "You needn't concern yourself."

Mike ignored her and looked at the child's finger. The fishing hook, a rusty barbed catfish hook, had gone in one side of the pad of her finger and out the other.

"Do you have something that will cut the barb off?" he asked, holding the little girl's hand gently.

Molly rummaged around in her tackle box and handed him a pair of small metal scissors. "I've also got a first-aid kit." She dove into a large picnic basket and removed a white tin box. "It's kind of like a credit card. With five kids, I never leave home without it." She handed him the kit.

"Could you move the rest of the kids back?" he asked impatiently. He wasn't accustomed to working with an audience.

"Maggie, you do what Mike tells you to do," Molly instructed, herding the rest of the kids away.

"Maggie—is that your name?" Mike asked the little girl as he carefully snipped off the barbed end of the hook.

She nodded her head, tears still streaking down her face.

"Did you know these hooks are for catching fish? This must be a pretty dumb hook, to mistake your finger for a fish. Your finger doesn't look anything like a fish."

A small smile tugged at the corners of her mouth. "Dumb old hook," she replied, then gasped as Mike quickly pulled it out. With an efficiency born from years of practice, Mike cleaned the wound and bandaged it. "There, all better," he pronounced as Molly came back to stand next to him. He looked at her and said, "Keep it clean and watch it for infection. Is she all caught up on her DPT shots?"

"Yes, she's current," Molly answered, giving Maggie a big hug.

Mike nodded and started to walk away.

"Mike?"

He paused and turned back to look at Molly.

"Thanks for your help."

He shrugged. "You brought me a pie, I bandaged a finger. I guess that makes us even." With these words, he walked away.

Molly watched him go, irritation mingling with curiosity.

She hadn't missed his annoyance when she and the kids had appeared. She grinned to herself, sitting back down on the soft grass. He cast murderous glares much better than he cast that spiffy fishing rod he had.

The man was a complete enigma. He had made his distaste for kids known in a dozen ways, yet he'd handled Maggie wonderfully. What had brought him out here from New York? He had the air of a man who would be more at home at the opera or the theater rather than a farm in the middle of Kansas.

Yes, the man was an interesting puzzle, and Molly had always enjoyed solving puzzles.

Chapter Three

"Don't let them talk you into staying up any later than ten. They've all had their baths and bedtime snacks." Molly grabbed her sweater and looked worriedly at the dark-haired woman who sat calmly at the kitchen table. "Scotty has the sniffles and I gave him some cold medicine, but you might want to give him some more before bedtime."

Leslie Winthrop gave Molly a tolerant smile. "Honestly, Molly, every time I baby-sit for you, you act as if I've never sat with the kids before." She stood up and directed Molly toward the front door with the delicacy of a bulldozer. "You haven't been out of this house to enjoy time for yourself in weeks. Now, go to the dance and enjoy."

Before Molly could voice any further instructions or hesitations, she found herself maneuvered out to the porch. She heard the click of the front door lock, then saw Leslie wave goodbye to her from behind the glass.

For a moment Molly stood hesitantly, wondering if it was a good idea for her to leave the kids for several hours. Scotty was definitely coming down with something. Jimmy had come home from school upset because he hadn't been chosen to play the role of Captain John Smith in the deaf children's school's fourth-grade play. Molly smiled at her own anxieties and got out her car keys. If she waited for when there were no personal crises and nobody was sick, she would have to wait for a very long time. Besides, medicine would fix Scotty up, and Molly was confident Leslie would be able to convince Jimmy that being an ear of corn in a human cornucopia was absolutely wonderful.

She climbed into the station wagon and turned on the ignition, holding her breath as the starter groaned in protest. "Come on," she muttered, pumping the gas pedal like a nurse administering CPR. With a backfire and a cough of the terminally ill, the engine roared to life.

"Add a new battery to the shopping list," she instructed herself, wincing as her shift into first gear was accompanied by a thump and grind. What she really needed was a new vehicle on her shopping list, but at the moment a new wagon wasn't at the top of her priorities—a room addition was. She had outgrown the three-bedroom farmhouse two kids ago. Of course, social services kept telling her they were finding permanent placements for the children who could be adopted, but if there was one thing she had learned in her eight years of foster parenting, it was that government agencies worked at the same pace as slugs on a cold morning. And they'd told her to expect another charge within a month.

As she drove past the Wiley place, her thoughts turned to her handsome neighbor. A week had gone by since the day they'd all shared the pond, and she'd seen nothing more of him. He still had her pie plate and she wondered if the reason he hadn't returned it was that he dreaded even a quick visit with her and the kids.

"I'll probably end up having to retrieve it myself," she muttered.

The drive into town took only fifteen minutes, and as she pulled into the lot of the community building where the dance was being held, a smile of anticipation curved her lips. She was looking forward to the evening. She loved to dance, and it had been a long time since she had attended one of these weekly gatherings.

Her anticipation was twofold. She was looking forward to the social aspect of the evening, but she was also hoping to get an opportunity to broach the subject of a loan for a room addition with Harvey Clemmons, her banker. She had learned in the past that Harvey was much more amenable when he had a couple shots of whiskey beneath his belt and the rhythm of the jukebox dancing in his veins.

She parked among the dozen trucks and cars already in the lot, then headed for the door of the community building. As she stepped inside, she was greeted by the sound of the jukebox pulsating with the latest tunes, the scent of the fresh sawdust that covered the floor, and the sight of freshly popped popcorn, which sat in huge bowls on the table.

"Molly, we're so glad to see you! It's been far too long since you've joined us for our Friday-night fun."

Molly smiled affectionately at the petite white-haired woman. Bess Walters was eighty years old, a widow with boundless energy who had been the guiding force behind the weekly dances. "I'm old, but I'm not dead," were Bess's favorite words.

"I decided to sneak away and enjoy the company of adults for the night," Molly explained.

"Huh, what you need is to sneak away and enjoy the company of a man," Bess exclaimed with a youthful twinkle in her blue eyes.

Bess laughed gleefully as Molly felt a slow blush paint her cheeks. "I don't need a man," she protested.

"Honey, nobody needs a man, but on a cold wintry night they are so much nicer than an electric blanket. And winter is coming."

Molly laughed and hugged Bess. "You are completely incorrigible."

"That's the nice thing about being old. You can be incorrigible and everybody writes it off to senility." Bess returned Molly's hug, then released her. "Now, go enjoy yourself."

As Molly walked across the room toward the makeshift bar in the corner, friendly smiles and inquiries about the children accompanied her. Oh, how she loved this small town where everybody knew everybody else and secrets were difficult to keep. She'd been to nightclubs in big cities, where you felt isolated and alone the moment you walked in the door. It was impossible to feel that way here; the townspeople were like an extended family. She got herself a cold beer, then sat down at one of the tables.

"Molly, how about a dance?"

She looked up and smiled into the face of a short squat older man, whose balding head gleamed from the lights above.

"Harvey, just the man I was looking for."

"Uh-oh, you've got that look in your eyes that usually costs me money." Harvey eyed her suspiciously as she stood up.

"Nonsense," Molly laughed. "I never cost you money. I only cost the bank money. If you'd go ahead and retire, you wouldn't have to put up with me and my financial problems."

"Huh, I'll retire the day they lay me in my coffin," he replied, putting an arm around her and moving her toward the dance floor. "I'm not about to leave my bank in the hands of the inexperienced. I've got almost forty years invested in it."

Molly smiled fondly as she followed his lead and listened to his familiar tirade. Harvey Clemmons was sixty-two, and the last thing he was ready for was retirement, a belief he was very vocal about. "Now I suppose you're going to make my life more miserable and ask me for another loan," Harvey finished.

"Harvey, I have a great idea for a room addition," Molly said, ignoring his groans as they moved across the dance floor.

As Mike headed his car into town, he was feeling inordinately pleased with himself. It had been a productive week. The moving van had arrived with his furnishings and he'd spent two days meticulously unpacking and rearranging until the house felt like home. He'd fixed the wobbly railing on the porch, repaired a broken shutter on a second-floor window, and the crowning glory had been the chopping down of a sickly tree into a neatly stacked load of split logs for firewood. He'd collapsed into bed each night, every muscle screeching in outrage at the unaccustomed abuse. But it had been good pain, proof of his changed life-style. And his badge of honor was the row of calluses decorating his palms.

It was pure impulse that spurred him to decide to go to the dance. He'd decided to reward his week of hard work with a little R and R. Besides, he wanted an opportunity to meet the people of Parsons, and he'd heard from the woman in the post office that these weekly dances were the best way.

His six-year-old Mercedes had been something of a joke among his friends back East, who believed in buying a new car every year. Mike was aware, as he pulled into the parking lot, that the car looked strangely foreign among all the pickups, Chevys and Fords.

As he got out of the Mercedes, he paused for a moment to look around. The lot was at the back of the community building, as were the parking areas for all the stores along Main Street.

Mike had driven through Parsons a year ago on his way to a conference in Oklahoma. He'd been immediately entranced with the small town. The business district was closed to traffic, and the street had been filled with fountains, benches and trees, creating the effect of an uncovered mall.

It had been this innovativeness and the open friendliness of the people that had drawn him back here when he had made the decision to leave New York.

With a smile of satisfaction, he walked into the building, immediately assailed by the sounds of music, talking and laughter.

"You must be the new man in town."

Mike looked down at an attractive white-haired woman. "Well, yes, I am new to the area. I'm Mike Wakefield."

"Bess Walters." Her intelligent frank blue eyes perused him from head to toe. "I'm not surprised you have all the unattached women whispering and primping. You're quite a handsome devil." She laughed as a deep blush stole over Mike's face. "Go on with you, give the ladies a thrill and go mingle."

What a spunky old woman, he mused, as he found a seat at one of the tables. Almost immediately his gaze found Molly. She was on the dance floor in the arms of a tall blond young man. For a moment Mike allowed himself the enjoyment of watching her moving with easy grace around the dance floor. Again, he was struck by Molly's wholesome attractiveness. Her shoulder-length hair fell in soft waves, gleaming with the brilliance of eighteen-karat gold beneath the overhead lights. She was wearing a deep-pink dress, cinched at the waist, the skirt flaring out to expose long shapely legs. Married legs, he reminded himself firmly.

He turned his attention to the man dancing with Molly. Her husband? Somehow Mike had expected Molly's husband to be stoop-shouldered and thin—tired from the strains of providing for their large family. However, this man looked young and carefree, and Mike felt an alien emotion flutter in his stomach as he saw the man throw his arms around Molly's shoulder with easy familiarity and lead her off the dance floor. Her gaze suddenly met his across the room. Embarrassed at having been caught staring, he quickly looked down at the tabletop, wondering idly who had carved the initials DJ into the wooden surface.

"Hi, enjoying yourself?" Molly had come over to where he sat.

"I'm not sure. I haven't been here long enough to know." Mike smiled up at her.

"May I join you?"

"Please." He gestured to the chair across from him.

Molly slid into it, then dipped her hand into the basket of popcorn that sat on the table. She popped a couple of pieces into her mouth and smiled. "I rarely make popcorn at home, and I never get it at the movies, but there's something about Bess's popcorn that's positively addicting."

"My personal choice at the theater is Milk Duds."

Molly shook her head, silken strands of hair shimmering like a gilded frame around her face. "You haven't lived until you watch a movie and indulge yourself with a bag of jujubes."

"Especially the red ones," Mike qualified.

"Especially the red ones," she agreed, a wide grin lighting her face. "This has got to be the most inane conversation I've had in weeks."

"It is a little ridiculous, isn't it?" He smiled back, and Molly noticed that his eyes were the deep green of a primeval forest. "I'd ask you to dance, but first I need to know if your husband is the jealous type."

"Gee, I don't know if he's the jealous type or not. I haven't met him yet." She laughed at the blank look that covered his face. "Mike, I'm not married."

"Not married?"

She shook her head.

"But . . . the children . . . ?"

She laughed again at his look of utter confusion. "Oh, Mike, I have a confession to make. The children aren't really mine. Three of them are foster kids, and the other two are children I baby-sit during the day."

"But, you said something about one on the way. You mean you're not . . . ?"

"No, I'm not. The agency is sending me another child. That's what I meant by one on the way."

"I just assumed . . ." He shook his head.

"I'm sorry," Molly apologized. "I let you assume."

"Molly, it's great to see you." A young woman with blazing red hair scooted into the chair next to Molly.

"Hi, Sally," Molly said in surprise. She and Sally Mayfield had gone to high school together but had never really been friends. Following high school, Molly had gone to the University of Kansas, and Sally had married her high-school sweetheart. She had divorced him two years earlier.

Molly and Sally hadn't exchanged more than fifteen words in the past couple of years.

"Aren't you going to introduce me to your friend?" Sally smiled coquettishly at Mike.

Of course, she should have known Sally's sudden friendliness had to do with the man sitting across from her, Molly thought. Sally was one of those predatory females who can smell an available man a mile away. Molly made the introductions.

"Janet, down at the post office, told me you're from New York. I've always wanted to go to New York. I went to Kansas City once. It was a high-school field trip. Remember, Molly, we went to the Museum of Natural History? It was a real bore, but I think most museums are boring, don't you?" She gave him no chance to reply as she batted her eyes and began another stream of prattle.

"I was always telling Bobby—that's my ex-husband—that we should leave this town and move to a big city, where they have more to offer for entertainment than these geriatric hoedowns."

Mike interrupted her before she could get a new burst of air. "Look, Sally," he said, "it's been really nice meeting you, but I promised Molly this dance."

"Oh, sure. Well, it was really nice to meet you, too. Maybe I'll stop by your place this week and bring you one of my famous chicken casseroles. You know, sort of as a welcome to the town."

"That would be great," Mike said, rising out of his chair and holding out his hand to Molly.

As they walked out on the dance floor, she grinned at him impishly. "You were beginning to get that look in your eyes that most men get after talking to Sally for a few minutes."

"What kind of a look is that?"

"Sort of a glazed bewilderment."

Mike chuckled. "Actually, I was wondering how it was physically possible for a woman to expel so much air without ever stopping to suck any in."

"It's a medical phenomenon nobody in Parsons has ever been able to figure out." She moved into his arms. The music was slow and she was instantly aware of several things. First and foremost was the fact that she found being in his arms tremendously pleasurable. Each breath she drew was filled with the scent of him, soap and shaving cream mingling with a subtle woodsy cologne. She'd forgotten how wonderfully accommodating the Creator had been when He made the differences between male and female physiques. It made dancing together so nice. She could feel the muscles of his shoulders beneath her fingertips, the warmth of his breath against her temple. She was aware of the strength of his long legs as he glided her expertly across the floor. With a sigh of contentment, she leaned her head against his chest and closed her eyes, giving herself to the moment, the music and the man.

Mike realized his arms had tightened involuntarily around her, pleasure flooding through him as she leaned her head against him. Funny, he had danced with Celia at least a thousand times, but he'd never felt as alive as he did at this moment, with Molly in his arms. She smelled good, like shampoo and sunshine and the subtle teasing whisper of flowers. He wondered briefly how she applied her perfume. Did she spritz it, or did she dab it on intimate places—behind her ears, at the back of her knees, between her breasts. This thought made the room seem suddenly unaccountably warm. He wasn't sure whether the heat was being radiated by his own thoughts or by Molly's nearness. There was relief mingled with disappointment as the song came to an end and she moved out of his arms.

"Thank you, you're a good dancer," she said as they walked back to the table.

"I've had a lot of practice. There was a time when it seemed like almost every evening I had some sort of charity dance to attend," Mike replied, thinking with distaste of all the stiff formal functions Celia had dragged him to over the years.

They were just about to sit down at the table when an elderly woman sitting nearby motioned them over. "Edna Warden, a lovely woman. Unfortunately she's

suffered a series of strokes that have left her para-
lyzed on one side,'' Molly whispered as they approached the woman. "Hello, Edna,'' she greeted
warmly, grasping her hand.

"Hello, Molly dear. I wanted you to introduce me
to your young man.'' Her voice was slightly slurred
and the left side of her face remained slack and mo-
tionless.

"This is Mike Wakefield,'' Molly said. "He just
recently moved into the Wiley place. Mike, Edna
Warden.''

"Mr. Wakefield, it's a pleasure to meet you and
welcome you to our town.'' She smiled at him warmly.
"You cut a fine figure on the dance floor. I used to do
quite a bit of dancing myself.'' Her voice was wistful.

Mike quickly assessed his own strength and the
frailty of the elderly woman. "Perhaps you'd do me
the honor of dancing the next dance with me.'' He was
vaguely aware of Molly's soft gasp.

"Oh, my, I couldn't do that...could I?'' Edna's soft
brown eyes looked at him hopefully.

"I don't see why you can't. Just put your right arm
around my neck and off we'll go.'' Edna followed his
instructions and Mike picked her up effortlessly and
moved her toward the dance floor.

Molly went back to the table and sat down, her gaze
lingering on Mike and Edna. Mike was talking to
Edna, a gentle smile on his face as he held the woman
up against him, her feet not touching the floor. Edna's face was radiant with joy as her head moved side
to side in time to the music.

He seemed so different tonight, she thought, comparing this man to the one she'd met on the two previous occasions. He seemed less uptight, more relaxed. She was delighted to discover that he had a good sense of humor. Watch yourself, old girl, she warned herself. There was nothing quite as appealing as a sexy handsome man who knew how to laugh.

As the music came to an end and Mike approached her table, she stood up. "I'd say you've earned yourself a drink. Why don't I show you where the bar is?"

"Great," he agreed, following her to the makeshift bar. It was a table, upon which sat a tub filled with ice and cans of soda and beer.

"What's your pleasure? Unfortunately, you don't have a lot of choices." She gestured to the tub.

"I'll take a beer." He moved to withdraw a wallet from his back pocket, but was stopped by Molly.

"It's on me," she said, paying for his and one for herself. With a warm smile, she handed him his beer. "Welcome to our town."

"Thank you." He accepted the can graciously. "How lucky can a man get? A can of beer from one beautiful woman and the promise of a famous chicken casserole from another."

"It may not be famous for the reasons you think." She giggled, thinking of the casserole that Sally brought to every function that required a covered dish.

"Uh-oh, that bad?"

"Let's just say different," she said diplomatically.

"What's in it?"

"That's a question that has confounded the residents of this town for years."

"I can't wait," he said wryly. Together they sat down at a table in the corner. They sipped their beers slowly, Mike's attention focused on the people on the dance floor and her attention focused on him. He looked about as in sync as a heavily dressed person at a nudist colony. Most of the men in the room wore flannel work shirts and worn jeans. Mike was wearing a pair of gray dress slacks with a gray pin-striped shirt.

Again she found curiosity prickling at her, like an itch that needed to be scratched. What was he doing out here in a little town like Parsons when he so obviously belonged in a big city? "So, what do you think of our social events? Probably nothing like what you're accustomed to in New York City."

"That's true," he answered thoughtfully. "This is a novel experience but one, I might add, I'm finding charming." A small smile curved his lips upward. "There seem to be some really colorful characters."

Molly laughed at his apt description. Yes, Parsons was full of colorful characters, all wonderfully warm, often eccentric people. "I'd say most small towns boast colorful characters. Big cities have them, too. They just get lost in the shuffle."

Mike smiled his agreement. "I got to the point where it seemed as if every colorful character in New York was personally trying to make my life miserable. I grew to hate the noise, the pace—everything."

"Hmm, sounds like a bad case of big-city burn-out."

He nodded thoughtfully. "I think that's exactly what I was suffering." Although it was much more than that, he left the subject alone, not wanting to delve deeper into his reasons for leaving.

"Mr. Wakefield?" Both Mike and Molly smiled as Bess approached their table. "I saw you out there cutting up the dance floor with Edna, and I think it only fair that you pass some of that talent around to some of us other women."

Mike laughed and got up from his chair. "I'd be delighted," he said, guiding the little woman onto the dance floor.

As the evening progressed, Molly continued to be surprised by Mike's patience and friendliness with everyone, particularly the older people. She found herself wondering if he exhibited the same patience in everything he did. Was he a patient lover? Were his caresses slow and languid, intended to evoke the sweetest of responses?

She was grateful for the chill night air that cooled her thoughts as she and Mike left the dance together at midnight.

"You made a lot of friends tonight," she said as he walked her outside. "You'll be the most popular man in town."

"I really enjoyed myself. Everyone is so friendly." He frowned as Molly stopped next to the driver's side door of her station wagon. "Molly, please tell me this hunk of junk isn't yours." He eyed the rusted banged-up wagon dubiously. "My God, does it really run?"

Molly laughed, her face lovely in the light of the brilliant moonlight. "Don't call Myrtle names. You'll offend her and she'll be difficult when I try to start her." She patted the side of the car gently. "Well, I guess this is good-night." She smiled up at him.

"Yes, I guess it is." He leaned against her car door, for some reason reluctant to have the evening end. He'd had a good time, the best he'd had in a very long while. And he owed much of the evening's enjoyment to Molly. He suddenly knew what would be a fitting ending to the pleasant evening. Her face registered surprise as he moved to cover her lips with his own. Her lips were soft and warm, as he had known they would be. He leaned into her, slipping an arm around her waist and pulling her closer as his tongue lightly flicked against her lips. He was achingly conscious of her full breasts pressing intimately against his chest, and desire flamed within him. He released her as abruptly as he had kissed her. "Good night, neighbor."

Molly's eyes were filled with confusion as she got into her car. By the time Mike had reached his Mercedes, Molly was pulling out of the parking lot.

He leaned against his car until the glow of her tail-lights were no longer visible, then he slid into the seat and stared thoughtfully at the dark dashboard.

Why had he done it? Why had he kissed her? Yet, even as he mentally voiced the question, he knew the answer. It had been a natural impulse. She'd looked so beautiful in the moonlight, and the kiss had seemed the only way to end a thoroughly enjoyable evening.

He'd been pleased to discover that, unlike most mothers, her conversation had not been inundated with amusing anecdotes of life with her kids. In fact, she hadn't mentioned them all evening, and they hadn't lacked for conversation.

She'd given him a taste of small-town life, and Mike in turn had described some of the unusual characters he encountered in his New York existence. He found himself exaggerating, stretching humorous stories just to evoke her laughter. Lord, he loved to hear her laugh. When Molly laughed, she held nothing back. The husky sound was full-bodied, coming from her toes, and he'd noticed that the sound of it made people around her smile with vicarious pleasure.

He sat up straighter in the driver's seat and started his engine. What on earth was he doing sitting in an empty parking lot in the middle of the night mooning about some woman? The last thing he needed or wanted was to get involved with a woman who had three kids and a decrepit station wagon named Myrtle.

Chapter Four

Molly's lips were still tingling as she steered the car toward home. Myriad emotions were buzzing around in her head creating utter chaos. "It was just a simple kiss," she chided herself, trying to negate the effect his lips had on her. "Just a simple meeting of two mouths." She lifted her fingertips to her lips and traced them, knowing no amount of rationalizations could take away the immeasurable flash of desire he had evoked in her. She'd been kissed a hundred times before, but no experience in her past had made her head spin like Mike's kiss had. She felt like a fairy princess who had received an enchanted kiss from a handsome prince.

She parked the car in front of the house and went inside. The house was quiet except for the low murmur of an old Bogart movie on television. Leslie was sprawled on the couch, Maggie asleep in her arms. With a finger to her lips to keep Molly quiet, Leslie untangled herself from the sleeping child and motioned Molly into the kitchen.

"Did Maggie give you a hard time?" Molly asked, sitting down with Leslie at the kitchen table.

"Nah, she never gives me a hard time. None of the kids do. She's always just a little anxious when you're not around."

Molly nodded thoughtfully. "I know. I just keep hoping she'll outgrow her fear of abandonment."

Leslie reached out and patted Molly's hand. "Give her time, Moll. She's still just a baby."

Molly nodded and smiled at Leslie. "Thanks for watching them. I don't know what I'd do without you. Finding a baby-sitter is hard when you're talking three kids."

Leslie shrugged. "I love kids. So, how was the dance?"

"Nice." Molly felt a warm blush cover her face as she thought of how wonderful dancing with Mike had been.

"Good, you needed a night out. A little time away from the kids makes a happy mom, and a happy mom makes a good one."

"And you deserve to be a mother more than anyone I know." Molly smiled sympathetically at her friend, who had been trying to get pregnant for the past two years.

"Well, actually, it looks like I'm going to get what you think I deserve." Leslie smiled excitedly. "As a matter of fact, the doctor tells me to expect an especially nice April Fool's Day surprise.''

"Oh, Leslie, that's wonderful!" Molly jumped up and gave her friend a hug of congratulations.

"I told Jim the other day that if I'd known it was going to take me so many years to get pregnant, he and I could have had a lot more fun in high school." Molly laughed as Leslie grinned wickedly.

"Well, it's wonderful news. Let me know if there's anything I can do."

"There is one little thing…" Leslie looked at Molly beseechingly. "Besides the fact that I'll need all the mother advice I can get, I'd kill for one of your baby quilts."

"You've got it. Just let me know when the time is right what colors you want it."

"Speaking of time…" Leslie looked down at her watch and jumped out of her chair. "I'd better scoot, or Jim will have the marines out looking for me. He seems to think that being pregnant is synonymous with being helpless."

"Then you'd better get home. I don't want the marines or Jim mad at me." Molly walked with her friend to the door. They exchanged another hug, then Molly watched as she got into her car and disappeared in the direction of town.

Lucky Leslie, Molly thought wistfully, staring blankly out her front door. She was married to a man who adored her, and finally, after years of trying, she was carrying the result of that love in her womb. Molly often allowed herself the fantasy of what her life would be like if she had a man to share it with.

Coffee for two in the mornings, whispered secrets at night. Yes, it would be wonderful to have a helpmate, a companion. The children fulfilled many needs in her, but she was aware of how many emotional and physical needs she'd tried to ignore for so long. She needed more than childish smooches and bear hugs. She was a healthy normal woman who needed more than what a bunch of children could offer her.

She wanted kisses that stirred her to her toes, slow languid caresses that would leave her begging for more. Mike's face suddenly flashed in her mind. She remembered the feel of his shoulder muscles beneath her fingertips, the length of his legs against her own as they had danced. She wondered what it would be like to feel him pressed tightly against her, both of them warm and naked beneath a layer of blankets....

She whirled away from the door, irritated by her fanciful thoughts. She was surely not the first woman to find Mike Wakefield attractive, and she certainly wouldn't be the last. She was allowing a simple neighborly kiss to feed fantasies that were far removed from reality.

She looked over to where Maggie was curled up asleep on the sofa. This was her reality—a child who suffered from nightmares and separation anxiety. Her world consisted of a barn that needed to be repainted and a house much too small for three children. She couldn't afford the time or energy it took to indulge in fantasies of romance with a handsome neighbor. She was being utterly ridiculous. This was a man who had been unpleasant more often than not, and had made it abundantly clear he didn't like kids.

Making sure Maggie was all right for the moment, Molly went into the bedroom to check on the boys. Thank goodness all three of the bedrooms were large, because every space was utilized. The boys' room held a set of bunk beds and two dressers, and one wall was covered completely in shelves to hold the treasures that young boys found so important—rock collections, a jar full of ants, a shoebox containing one fat toad. The shelves had, at one time or another, held everything a boy might find near and dear.

A soft smile curved Molly's lips as she tucked Scotty's arm beneath the blanket and took a plastic truck away from Jimmy before checking to make sure his bed was still dry.

She went back into the living room and picked up Maggie. "Come on, Bean, it's time to get back into bed."

"I had a bad dream, Molly." She snuggled closer, molding her wiry form into Molly's curves.

"Bad dreams are all gone now," Molly said, kissing Maggie's forehead. "See, I kissed them all away." Molly carried the little girl into the smallest of the bedrooms, where a trundle bed was waiting to receive her. She lay Maggie down and pulled the blankets up around her neck. She started to leave the room, but paused at the doorway, looking back at Maggie. Snuggled beneath the covers, thumb like a protruding extension of her mouth, she was fast asleep. Molly smiled, a loving smile of tenderness. Always before, she had managed to maintain a certain modicum of emotional distance from the kids she fostered, a necessary distance because she so often had to tell the kids goodbye. But Maggie was different. Maggie, with her little tough-guy veneer hiding a fear of abandonment, had managed to crawl right into the core of Molly's heart. Maybe it was because Maggie reminded Molly so much of herself as a child.

As Molly crawled into bed, she thought of her earlier daydreams of love. Fantasies are for children, she decided, then smiled. Still, it would be nice. . . .

"Harvey, that's only a third of what I need to build a new room." Molly's face registered dismay as she looked at the man seated behind the desk.

"I know Molly, but I don't know what else I can do for you. I'm finagling figures just to get you that much." Harvey looked at her sympathetically. "Molly, the house is mortgaged to the hilt. You've seen the paperwork." He gestured to the mound of papers on the desk before him. Molly nodded dismally. She and Maggie had driven into the bank as soon as the kids had gotten on the school buses, and they had been there ever since, as Molly and Harvey worked and reworked figures that simply wouldn't add up to what Molly needed. "I'm sorry, there's just nothing more I can do."

"Can we go now?" Maggie asked. Her level of patience had been reached and surpassed long ago. She kicked the desk with the toe of a scuffed tennis shoe.

"In a minute, and don't kick the desk," Molly replied absently, her mind whirling desperately. "What about the station wagon? The title is clear on it. Couldn't you give me a couple thousand more using it as collateral?"

Harvey gave her a pained look. "Molly, you couldn't use that piece of junk as collateral for a cup of coffee." He sighed heavily. "Okay, okay. I'll give you another two thousand using the wagon as collateral."

Molly jumped out of her chair, leaned over the desk and planted a kiss right in the middle of Harvey's bald head. "Thanks, Harvey. You really do have a heart."

"If this gets around town, everyone will think I've blown a gasket," he muttered, pulling out the necessary paperwork.

Molly laughed. "I promise I won't tell anyone."

"Hmph, the last time somebody told me that, it was all over town that I was wearing boxer shorts with little bunnies on them." Harvey grinned, then looked at her seriously. "So what are you going to do? You still don't have the money to have the room built."

"No, but I'll work it out some way. I really need that extra room." Molly grinned at Harvey reassuringly. "Don't worry, Harvey. I've got it all figured out. You know Tom Currothers, Carrie's dad? He's a contractor. He's promised me that he'll do most of the work at a discount. I was going to have him do the whole thing, but now I'll have him rough it in and I can do the finish work myself."

It took another half hour for Molly to sign all the necessary paperwork, then she and Maggie left the bank with a cashier's check tucked securely in her purse.

"Now, we need to go over to Currothers' Builders so I can talk to Tom about this project. I just hope he was serious when he made the offer of building the room for a reasonable amount of money."

"Molly, I'm hungry!" Maggie exclaimed, pulling Molly from her thoughts.

She looked at her watch in startlement. "Heavens, it's after noon. No wonder you're hungry. How about lunch at Wanda's?"

"Yea!" Maggie agreed with a wide grin.

Wanda's Café was a favorite eating place for most of the townsfolk, but especially for Molly's kids, who adored not only the sweet concoctions the café was noted for, but also Wanda herself.

"There's my little plum pudding." Wanda swooped Maggie up in her ample arms the minute Molly and Maggie entered the café.

"Hi, Wanda." Molly smiled as the woman pretended to bite Maggie's nose, making the little girl giggle with delight. "Got a table for two for lunch?"

"I think that can be arranged," Wanda replied. "Follow me." She turned and led Molly toward the back of the restaurant.

Wanda was a walking advertisement for her own culinary skills. As wide as she was tall, she had a broad face that beamed with good humor and a candid tongue that loved to gossip.

"Here we are, the best seat in the house," she said, depositing Maggie on one of the chairs at a small table. "And I happen to have baked a chocolate cream pie this morning, and it's back there just waiting for a little girl who loves chocolate."

"I do!" Maggie exclaimed. "I love chocolate."

"Well now, imagine that." Wanda grinned. "We'll just have to see that you get an extra-big piece—that is, after you eat a good lunch." She winked broadly at Molly. "And what's this I hear about you dancing up a storm Saturday night with a certain handsome new man in town?"

"Don't believe any of it," Molly laughed, knowing the gossipmongers of Parsons were alive and extremely verbal. Molly quickly gave Wanda their lunch order, wanting to stem the woman's penchant for gossip. She hoped that by the time they ate she would still have time to run the rest of her errands before four o'clock, when the buses brought the other kids home from school.

"Molly."

They all turned to see Mike, who had just entered the café and was heading for their table.

"Uh-oh, it's the grouch," Maggie uttered softly.

"Shh," Molly hissed, then smiled up at him. "Hi, Mike."

"Molly, aren't you going to introduce me?" Wanda asked, eyeing Mike as if he were a plump juicy pork chop.

Molly made the introductions, then gestured Mike into the chair across from her. "Would you like to join us?'' She had no control over the way her heart beat more rapidly as she looked at him. This was the first time she'd seen him since Saturday night at the dance, since his kiss, and as always he looked magnificent. He had succumbed to country life and was wearing a pair of jeans that fit him as if he'd been born in them. He'd looked great in dress slacks, but she was pleased to notice that he looked equally at ease in jeans and a plaid flannel shirt.

''No, thank you.'' His voice was stiffly formal and she noticed for the first time that his eyes were a cold granite gray. There was no hint of the responsive green hues that had warmed her on the night of the dance. *Uh-oh, here comes the grouch,* she thought, silently echoing Maggie.

''I went by your house this morning, but you weren't home.''

''I've been in town all morning.'' Molly gestured to the chair once again. ''Please,'' she said, not wanting the psychological disadvantage of his hovering over her while she sat.

He reluctantly sat down, then looked up at Wanda, who was watching them both with ill-concealed interest. ''I don't care for anything to eat, but I would like a cup of coffee.'' He smiled pointedly at the plump proprietor until she moved away from the table to fill their orders. Mike turned his attention back to Molly. ''I saw your car outside and knew I'd find you in here.''

''So you did. What's up?'' Molly asked guardedly, her tone reminiscent of a tiptoe through a mine field.

He sighed heavily, running a hand through his dark hair. "It's about your kids."

She stiffened defensively. "What about them?"

He looked pained, as if he'd rather be anywhere in the world but here having this conversation. "I think they've been causing some mischief over at my place."

"What kind of mischief?" She asked, disbelieving. She'd had kids in the past who were difficult, children who demanded a firm hand, an extra measure of patience. But the kids in her care now were not the type to make devilment.

"I think they've been overturning my garbage, strewing it all over the yard." She stared at him skeptically as he continued. "Look, I know it doesn't sound like much, but I'm afraid if you let this go, they'll just see it as a green light to make more mischief. You know kids—give them an inch and they'll take a mile."

"You don't like kids very much, do you?" She voiced the suspicion she'd had since she'd first met him.

He flushed, his gaze not quite meeting hers. "My personal feelings on that topic have nothing to do with this." He leaned forward across the table. "Maybe they're trying to pay me back for yelling about the barn. Maybe they're angry because I'm not letting them use it as their clubhouse. Maybe they just consider it some sort of practical joke, but I don't find it amusing."

"My kids wouldn't do something like that." Her voice was flat and certain.

Mike looked at her tolerantly, a look that infuriated her. "Molly, we live out in the middle of nowhere. It *has* to be your kids." His face flushed again, this time with the beginnings of anger. "It's a childish sort of thing to do and your kids are the only children around for miles." His mouth was a taut line of impatience. "The bags were tied up and left right outside the house. I'm telling you, it *had* to be your kids."

"And I'm telling you it's not," Molly returned heatedly. "I know my kids and they wouldn't do something like this. And I find it deplorable that just because you don't like kids you're using mine as scapegoats for your city stupidity." She glared at him with all the ferocity of a mother lion protecting her cubs.

"And just what is that supposed to mean?" Mike lowered his voice as he realized they were drawing the unwanted attention of fellow diners.

"Anyone who leaves their garbage outside in plastic bags deserves to have it thrown all over their yard," she retorted.

"Well, I didn't know I was moving next door to Ma Barker and her gang of juvenile delinquents."

Molly bit back an angry reply, aware of Maggie's fascinated gaze studying both her and Mike. "This is getting out of hand," she said after taking a steadying breath. "If you want to catch the real culprits, then I suggest you sit up and watch your garbage all night."

"And I suggest you sit up all night and watch to see who's sneaking out of your house to cause me problems.'' He stood up, a glower marring his handsome features.

"Good day, Mr. Wakefield," Molly said, her tone cold.

"Good day, Ms. Smith," he returned just as frigidly.

"Damn!" he exploded the moment he stepped outside the café. He couldn't remember a time when he'd allowed a woman to upset him more. He'd liked her, had been attracted to her warmth and humor last Saturday night, but the bitter taste of disillusionment burned in his mouth. She was exactly like so many other mothers he'd dealt with in the past, prejudicially blind to the faults of her children. "There must be some mistake, Dr. Wakefield—my Johnny wouldn't bite you." Or, "Oh, you must be mistaken, Dr. Wakefield—my little Willy would never kick a nice man like you." Oh, yes, Mike had had his fill of denials from mothers of monsters.

When he'd awakened yesterday morning and discovered his garbage strewn all over the ground, his first thought had been Molly's kids. He'd decided to write it off as an isolated incident and forget about it. But when he got up this morning and saw that the offense had been repeated, he'd decided to speak to Molly. After all, what did she really know about the children she was fostering?

He got into his car and sat for a few minutes, allowing his anger to work through him. His reasons for going to Molly had been twofold. He wanted the mischief stopped, but more importantly, he wanted her to be aware that it was possible one or more of her kids were sneaking out of the house. He didn't like the idea of a child wandering around in the dead of night—it was potentially dangerous.

Still, he was disappointed in Molly's reaction. He'd expected some disbelief, but not the shakeless vehement denial she'd exhibited. For some reason he had expected more from her.

"City stupidity, indeed," he muttered irritably, starting his engine with a roar. He'd show her. Tonight he'd sit up all night if necessary. He'd catch the guilty culprits and march them over to her. He grinned, almost able to hear Molly's heartfelt apology ringing in his ears.

Chapter Five

"Hello?" Mike picked up the telephone receiver as he poured water into the coffee maker.

"Well, darling, it's been nearly a week. Are you ready to admit defeat and return to urban pleasures?"

"No way," Mike replied, recognizing Celia's voice. "I was just making myself a pot of coffee."

"Coffee? At this hour? You'll be up all night."

"That's the idea," he said, sitting down at his glass-topped kitchen table. "I have a mission to accomplish tonight."

"Indeed, sounds fascinating! Tell me more."

"It's a long story, one you would probably find extremely boring." Mike knew with certainty that Celia would find everything about Molly and her kids tedious, just as she had always found his talking about his work with young patients. It was for this same reason that he hadn't told her when things about his work had begun to turn sour for him. He hadn't mentioned the final straw that had broken his back and made him decide to get away from his practice for a while.

"So, what are you doing for social activity? I suppose square dances and barn raisings are a dime a dozen. Personally, I can't imagine you do-si-do-ing with some farmer's daughter." There was an arch sarcasm in her voice, one he'd always found rather amusing, but now found slightly irritating.

"Actually, I went to a dance the other night at the community center, and I had a wonderful time."

"Meet anyone interesting?" Now her voice had a studied nonchalance.

"I met a lot of fascinating people. There's Bess, the youngest eighty-year-old woman I've ever known. Then there's Sam Edwards. He owns the hardware store and claims to be a direct descendant of Benjamin Franklin." He went on to mention some of the other colorful characters he'd met since moving to Parsons. It wasn't until after he and Celia had hung up that he realized he hadn't mentioned Molly. It was almost as if he'd consciously made a decision to keep the women in his life totally separate.

"That's a stupid thought," he muttered aloud, getting up from the table and pouring himself a cup of coffee. Celia was a good friend, an undemanding companion and at times a confidante, but he'd certainly never considered her in a romantic light. And Molly...Molly certainly wasn't the woman in his life.

Granted, she was extremely attractive, and a very pleasant dance partner, but she could never be anything more than that to him.

"And she's a self-righteous, overprotective..." he let the words die on his lips as he contemplated the night to come. He was still stinging from the conversation with her earlier in the day. If he had to sit up every night for the next month, he'd catch the trash throwers and prove to her that kids were nothing but trouble.

Armed with a healthy dose of determination and a powerful flashlight, he planted himself at the darkened living-room picture window. From this vantage point he could just make out the shadowy forms of the huge green plastic bags by the edge of the porch. When he saw something suspicious, all he'd have to do was yank open the front door and shine his light. He grinned to himself. He felt like a Midwestern Rambo, waiting for an attack from hostile foreign forces. Only in this case, the foreign forces were all under four feet tall and were probably armed with spitballs. And the kids today don't even know how to make decent spitballs, he mused, leaning comfortably back in his chair.

Molly—it was amazing how much time and energy he'd expended in thinking about her since the night of the dance. On the one hand he'd been disturbed by the presence of her kids—three of them, for God's sake, and that wasn't counting the ones she baby-sat on a regular basis. They represented everything he'd tried to leave behind. On the other hand, he couldn't seem to forget the way she had felt in his arms when they had been dancing. The memory of her breasts pressing against his chest, her heartbeat conversing with his own, had the capacity to stir his desire for her. And when they had kissed, her lips warmly pliant beneath his, a tenderness was elicited that only served to intensify his desire.

But Mike wasn't looking for a relationship. He'd come to Kansas to find himself, to discover if he had what it took to be Dr. Michael Wakefield, pediatrician. The last thing he needed was involvement with Molly to complicate his life. With this thought firmly in mind, he directed his stare out the window.

He awoke with a start, appalled that he'd fallen asleep. Some Rambo he'd make. His eyes instantly sought the front yard. Adrenaline spurted through him as in the shadows of the night he made out furtive movement. Triumph coursed through him as he saw that the shadowy shapes were small—the size of children. He got up out of his chair and stealthily made his way to the front door. Aha! He'd catch the little stinkers and march them right over to Molly's place. Taking a deep breath, he yanked open the door and leapt out, simultaneously turning on the flashlight.

For a moment the culprits froze, as if blinded by the intense glare of the unexpected light. A spontaneous yell of surprise left Mike's mouth as he stared at two of the biggest raccoons he'd ever seen in his life. His yelp broke the stunned inertia of the creatures and they scurried away, leaving in their wake a trail of discarded cans, meat wrappers and spoiled vegetables.

"I'll be damned," Mike said slowly, thoughts of Molly's imagined humble apology dissolving. City stupidity. He grinned. Maybe he had a lot more to learn about country living than he'd thought.

"Molly, I can't find my shoe."

"I need an extra dollar today for the field trip. My dad forgot to give it to me before he brought me this morning."

Molly, still clad in pajamas and bathrobe, raced from one crisis to the next. No matter how early she got up, no matter how organized she thought she was, the fifteen minutes before the school buses arrived always disintegrated into mobocracy. She found the missing shoe under the sofa, then grabbed her purse to get a dollar.

She'd just finished recombing Carrie's hair when she became aware of a soft knock at the door. Probably one of the bus drivers, who often had to come in for their little passengers.

"It's open!" Molly yelled, at the same time blowing strands of her hair out of her face. She froze as Mike stuck his head in the door.

"Bad time?"

Bad time, Molly mused dismally. She'd hardly had a chance to drink her morning coffee. She looked like a clown who had just been exploded out of a cannon. This was the most harried part of her day, when she was trying not only to get her own kids ready for school, but also the two she baby-sat, who arrived at her house early each morning.

She hesitated, then shook her head. "I'll be with you in just a minute," she said, her hand unconsciously moving to smooth down her hair. All thoughts of Mike flew out of her head as she heard the squeak of bus brakes outside.

"There's the bus," Maggie said from her seat on the sofa by the window. She looked over to where Mike stood awkwardly just inside the front door. "You'd better sit down over here," she instructed, patting the sofa next to her. "You're gonna get runned over."

Mike decided to take the little girl's advice and he sat down next to her on the worn sofa. He watched with interest as Molly distributed what he assumed were sack lunches. Along with a lunch, she gave each girl a kiss and a special word of goodbye, and sent them out the door to the waiting bus. She'd no sooner got them out the door when another smaller bus pulled up and Scotty and Jimmy were sent out the door, with Molly following closely to wave from the front porch.

Suddenly the house was silent. "Is it always like this in the mornings?" Mike asked, as Molly came back into the house.

Molly started to make some sort of protest, but Maggie beat her to it.

"Yup," she answered.

Molly nodded agreement, realizing it was useless to pretend that her life with the kids was anything other than what it was. Then, remembering the unpleasantness of her last conversation with Mike, she smiled at Maggie. "Bean, why don't you go get dressed." She waited until the little girl had left the room, then she looked at Mike speculatively. "What are you doing here, anyway?"

He smiled sheepishly and held out her pie plate. "I wanted to return this to you. I was going to refill it before I brought it back, but I didn't know the exact ingredients of humble pie."

"I don't understand."

Mike stood up from the sofa, a pained expression on his face. "I sat up last night to catch whoever was ripping into my garbage."

"And?" Molly tried to hide a grin, able to guess what he had discovered.

"And, unless your kids grow fur after dark and wear Zorro masks, I owe you a big apology."

"Yes, you do," she agreed smugly.

"You aren't going to let me off easily, are you?" He looked at her with a small grin. "I suppose you want to see me grovel."

"Groveling is nice," she agreed complacently. She giggled as he suddenly threw himself down on one knee.

"Please, Molly, forgive me. I guess it's part of my big-city paranoia. I never considered that it might be some kind of animal. Please, tell me you forgive me." One of his dark eyebrows shot up and a grin lifted one corner of his mouth. "Enough?"

"More than enough." She laughed. "Would you like a cup of coffee?"

"I'd love one—groveling always makes me thirsty." He got up and followed her into the big country kitchen.

The room was the heart of Molly's home, but as Mike stood hesitantly in the doorway, she realized that at the moment the room resembled the aftermath of a tornado.

The spaciousness was reduced somewhat by the huge table covered with the remains of a scrambled-egg breakfast. The portable color television on top of the refrigerator was still playing the last of the morning cartoons. With a smile, she reached up and shut it off. "Uh, have a seat." She gestured at the kitchen table. Then, embarrassed by the dirty dishes on the tabletop, she hurriedly began stacking them in the sink. "I apologize for the mess, but mornings are always rather hectic around here. The kids I baby-sit arrive early, so getting five kids ready and off to school is the most difficult feat I accomplish all day long." She flushed slightly, realizing she was rambling.

"Molly, don't apologize," he said softly. "I dropped in unexpectedly and I should have realized you'd be busy with the children." He picked up a plate and a glass and added it to the stack in the sink.

"Oh, please, you don't have to do that," she protested as he picked up more dirty dishes.

"I don't mind." He smiled at her. "Besides, I have a feeling you won't sit down and share a cup of coffee with me until the dishes are scraped and in the dishwasher." He handed her a plate. "You scrape and I'll finish clearing the table."

She started to protest, but Mike stopped her. "Please, Molly. Consider it part of my groveling."

She nodded and took the plate from him.

In the next few minutes she felt as if her kitchen had physically shrunk. Mike seemed to fill the room with his presence. No matter what she did, he seemed to be too close to her, his broad shoulder brushing hers, their hands meeting over a dirty plate or cup. His fragrance surrounded her, the clean male scent that made her blood course a little more quickly through her veins.

He seemed to be a different man from the grave uptight one who'd confronted her about the boys' using his barn. She'd first noticed the difference the night of the dance, and it was just as apparent today. He was more relaxed, his smiles coming more quickly. He appeared...happier, and it made him all the more appealing.

She was almost relieved when the dishwasher was humming in the background and the width of the table was between Mike and herself.

"Cream or sugar?" she asked, pushing the creamer and sugar bowl toward him.

"No, thanks. I take mine black." He took a sip from his cup and smiled at her. He knew she was embarrassed by her appearance. It was obvious by the way she kept running her hands through her hair and belting and rebelting the pink velour robe. Yet Mike thought he had never seen anyone look lovelier. Granted, her hair was in soft disarray, but it gave her a just-loved aura that was extremely sexy. The robe, rather than hiding her curves, emphasized the soft fullness of her breasts, the rounded lines of her hips. It was easy to imagine swooping her up in his arms and carrying her into the bedroom, where her bed would still be warm and inviting.

"Molly, I can't do these up." Maggie came into the kitchen, the shoulder straps of her overalls trailing down her back. Mike's erotic images vanished like a startled bird taking flight.

"Come on, I'll help." Molly's face was lit with her obvious affection for the little girl as she fastened the straps of the overalls. For a split second Mike wondered what it would be like to have that same look in her eyes when she gazed at him. He took a large drink of his coffee, gasping as the hot liquid burned the insides of his mouth.

"Hot," he hissed to Maggie and Molly.

"Molly says you shouldn't gulp your drink." Maggie proclaimed, eyeing Mike solemnly. "She says it's rude. That makes you a rude grouch."

"Maggie," Molly gasped in horror, feeling her face turn crimson with embarrassment. She looked at Mike helplessly, relieved to see a small smile on his face.

"I think that's my cue to get back home." He got up from his chair, his attention drawn to a quilting rack in the corner of the room. He paused and looked at the partially finished patchwork quilt. "Molly, did you do this?" He bent closer and eyed the small uniform stitches. "This is beautiful work." Admiration shone in his eyes.

"Thank you. I enjoy doing it."

"My mother is really into quilts. Do you sell them when you're finished?"

"Sometimes, but usually I give them to friends as gifts." She smiled crookedly. "That particular quilt is my family quilt."

"Family quilt?" He looked at her quizically.

She walked over and stood next to him, running her hand lovingly over the material. "Each child that comes to stay with me chooses a piece of material and I add it to this quilt." She smiled at Mike. "You put all these little pieces of material together and you get a quilt. You take children from all over the country and send them to me and we make a family, sort of a patchwork family." She shrugged and laughed self-consciously.

"It's really lovely," he said, complimenting her. "Well, thanks for the cup of coffee." He opened the front door, then looked back at her curiously. "There's a huge lumber truck pulling up out front."

"Oh, no! I didn't think they'd be here so early." She looked at him frantically. "I can't go out there now, not in my robe—not with you here." She flushed as he looked at her inquiringly. "Mike, Parsons is a very small town, and one of the characteristics of a small town is a very strong grapevine. These men will go back into town and tell somebody you were here and I was in my robe, and by the time the rumor makes its rounds, the tale will be that you were chasing me naked around the barn."

Mike grinned wickedly and Maggie followed his example, not wanting to be left out of the conversation. "You want me to sneak out the back door?" he asked.

"No. Would you go out and tell them to unload the material and stack it in the barn? I'll run in and get dressed." Without waiting for an answer, she whirled around and disappeared into the bedroom.

She dressed quickly in jeans and a sweatshirt, pulled a brush through her hair, then ran outside, where Mike and four young men from the lumberyard were nearly finished unloading the truck.

"I didn't mean for you to stay and help," she protested, helping Mike pick up a four-by-eight-foot piece of plasterboard.

"I don't mind," he replied, as they dragged the board along the ground and stacked it on top of the pile already in the barn.

Within fifteen minutes the truck was unloaded, and Mike, Molly and Maggie watched it pull away.

"What's all this for?" Mike asked as the truck disappeared from sight.

"We're going to build on a room." Molly answered absently, her mind whirling over the materials she'd seen unloaded to make sure everything had been delivered.

"Who's we?" He followed her into the barn.

"Did you see the roofing shingles?"

"Over there." He pointed to the paper-wrapped shingles "Who's we?" He repeated.

"Huh? Oh, actually, I mean me." She walked around a pile of two-by-fours. "Did you see a box of ten-penny nails?"

"We stacked the boxes of nails against the wall over there." He grabbed her by the shoulders. "Molly, stop your inventory for a minute." She looked up at him. "What do you mean you're going to build a room?

You can't do that. Why didn't you hire a contractor?''

"I have. Tom Currothers, Carrie's dad. He's a builder and he's agreed to put up the room. Just the shell, then I can do all the finish work.''

"That's the most illogical thing I've ever heard,'' Mike said, impatience deepening his voice. He was appalled at the thought of her hefting plasterboard and lugging lumber. "You can't finish a room all by yourself.''

"Yes, I can,'' she returned. "Besides, it's really not your problem.''

"Molly, do you realize how much work is involved just to finish a room? You're talking about drywalling and painting, not to mention wiring.''

"A little hard work doesn't scare me.'' She lifted her chin in a show of defiance.

"Let me help you,'' he offered.

"Don't be silly,'' she scoffed.

"I'm not being silly, I'm being perfectly serious. I worked for a construction company while I was earning money for medical school. Together you and I can get a lot done while the kids are in school.''

"Are you telling me you possess carpentry skills?'' She eyed him, dubious about his building abilities.

"I know my way around with a hammer and nails,'' he said with a hint of modesty.

"Still, I can't let you do that. I can't pay you anything, and I won't accept charity.'' Her chin rose a fraction of an inch higher.

"Make me a quilt,'' he said impulsively. "I'll help you build your room and you can repay me by making me one of your hand-sewn quilts.'' She still hesitated. "Please, Molly, it's the neighborly thing to do," he said insistently.

"Okay—your labor for one of my quilts." She held out her hand. As they shook on the deal, Molly smiled. Maybe this was a good idea. Maybe when he spent some time with all the kids, he'd realize they weren't so bad after all. She liked the idea of Mike's being here during the days, then staying and sharing their evening meal, presiding over them all from the head of the table. She liked Mike and she wanted him to like not only her, but her family, as well. Yes, this just might be the start of something wonderful.

Mike released Molly's hand with a jaunty grin. He liked Molly, and he was looking forward to spending time with her, even if it meant working together to build a room. He could arrive in the mornings after the school buses left and leave before the buses brought the kids home. Maggie wasn't too bad to have around. Besides, didn't children her age take naps? This was perfect. He could spent time with Molly without the infernal presence of those kids. His grin widened. Oh, yes, this could be the start of something wonderful.

Chapter Six

There was a jaunty swagger to Mike's gait as he covered the distance from his place to Molly's. It was another picture-perfect autumn day, with brilliant red and gold leaves creating colorful canopies overhead. The sun was as warm as a lover's touch on his back, and a sense of adventure buoyed his spirits as he anticipated the day to come.

It was funny, really, how much he was looking forward to this project of helping Molly finish her room addition. Every day for the past week he had made a point of driving by her place, watching the progress of the workers as the foundation was laid, then the room framed in. Yesterday he'd watched from a distance as they completed their work and loaded up their trucks, then he'd called Molly and made arrangements to help her this morning.

Mike looked forward to the challenging physical elements of the job. He anticipated the pleasure of having something to do to fill the hours of the days. Back in New York, time had flown on speedy wings as his medical practice took up all his waking hours. Here, with very little he could do on the farm, there was too much time to think, too much time to dwell on memories that made him ache deep within.

Yes, he was hungry for physical activity. He'd even dressed the part of a laborer, donning a worn pair of jeans and a flannel work shirt. He'd completed his casual outfit with a New York Yankees baseball hat he hadn't worn in years. A hammer hung from his belt, completing the picture of macho competence. He felt younger, more carefree than he had in a long time.

He looked at his wristwatch and smiled in satisfaction. Just after eight. The kids would all be gone, whisked away to school for the day. Thank heaven for the Department of Education. That left only the little minx Maggie to contend with, and he was hoping that by noon the little girl would be in for a nap and he could spend some time alone with Molly.

It wasn't that he was entertaining lewd and lustful thoughts of Molly—although he had to admit he wouldn't mind holding her in his arms once again, breathing in her wholesome fragrance, tasting the honeyed sweetness of her lips. The thought quickened his pace.

Anticipation carried him quickly across the front yard and up to her porch, where he knocked a cheerful staccato.

Maggie opened the door, a thumb in her mouth, and her other hand holding the unfastened snap of one of the shoulder straps of her overalls. "Molly says come in and have a cup of coffee. She'll be out in a minute."

Mike followed the little girl into the kitchen where he helped himself to a cup of coffee, then sat down at the table.

Maggie stood right next to him, eyeing him with her solemn blue eyes. "You have cracks in your face," she observed, popping her thumb out of her mouth.

"What?"

"By your eyes." She reached up and touched the lines that radiated from the outer corners of his eyes. "Cracks."

Her hand was small and cool to the touch, reminding him of all the wonder he used to find in the magic of children. Each time he'd held a baby in his arms, doctored a cut or a scrape on a toddler's knee or elbow, he'd been struck by the miracle of youth, of innocence. Now, the miracle was tainted, destroyed by a single incident that had marked him forever.

"They're wrinkles," he explained gruffly, glad when she removed her little hand from his face. "You get them when you're frustrated. Kids gave them to me."

"Oh." She watched silently as he took a sip of his coffee, then moved closer to him. "I can't get my overalls hooked." She looked at him expectantly.

"Molly will fix you up when she comes out." He took another sip of his coffee, trying to ignore the steady blue gaze that penetrated him. It was slightly disconcerting, the way kids had of looking you right in the eyes, as if they were able to see things deep in your soul that nobody else could see.

"Molly's busy with Scotty."

"What's wrong with Scotty?" Mike asked, remembering him as the red-haired freckle-faced boy he'd first encountered in his barn.

"He threw up."

Concern for the boy immediately flooded through Mike, followed by the knowledge that if it was anything serious Molly would have called him. It's a conspiracy, Mike thought, as his plans to spend some time alone with Molly went up in a puff of smoke.

"So can you hook my pants?"

With an inward sigh, he grabbed the fastening and tried to fit it over the large brass button. He worked with it for several seconds, growing more frustrated as the button remained elusive.

"Molly can do it real fast."

"Well, the damn thing's tricky!" he exclaimed. "There," he added when he was finally successful. "Is Molly with Scotty now?"

Maggie nodded, the thumb relodging in her mouth.

"Aren't you afraid that one of these days you'll suck that thumb right off your hand?"

A small smile curved her lips up on either side of the thumb. "Thumbs don't come off."

Mike grinned at her. "I guess you're right. Why don't you take me to Scotty and Molly."

She nodded and held out her free hand to him. Mike hesitated, then took it, his heart constricting as he felt her small trusting grasp.

She led him to a bedroom, where he found Molly standing next to a set of bunk beds, Scotty on the top bunk.

He hesitated in the doorway, not wanting to intrude but wanting to help if he could. "Molly?"

She turned at the sound of his voice, her face lighting with a smile that warmed his heart. "Mike, I'm sorry. I sent Maggie down to let you in, but I didn't hear you arrive." She looked back at the sick boy. "Scotty decided he didn't like my breakfast this morning."

Scotty managed a weak smile.

"I think it must be the flu," Molly continued. "There's a lot going around school."

"Fever?" Mike walked over to the bunk, noticing the paleness that made Scotty's freckles seem to stand out in bas-relief.

"A little, but I gave him some acetaminophen."

Mike lay his hand on Scotty's forehead, his other hand automatically moving to press gently on the little boy's stomach. "Does his tummy hurt?"

Molly signed Mike's question to Scotty, who nodded and signed his answer.

"He says he feels like he's going to be sick."

"Definitely sounds like a flu bug. He'll probably be fine by tomorrow," Mike said.

"See, you'll be fine. Even Mike agrees." Molly assured Scotty, signing, then gently stroking his forehead. "Try to sleep and you'll feel better when you wake up. The bell is here." She pointed to a small bell on the bed next to him. "You ring it if you need anything, okay?"

He nodded and closed his eyes. Molly, Maggie and Mike all left the bedroom.

"Would it be better if I come back tomorrow to start on the room?" Mike asked as they all went into the kitchen.

"No, Scotty should be fine. He'll probably sleep for most of the day." She smiled, a quicksilver flash of her irrepressible humor. "Besides, we're both dressed in our working finery." She struck a model's pose, exhibiting her worn jeans with threadbare knees and her paintstained sweatshirt. Mike thought she looked adorable, with the jeans hugging her inviting curves and the pink sweatshirt loving her firm breasts.

"It's exactly what all the fashion designers were showing back in New York," he teased.

"What about me?" Maggie emulated Molly's pose, making both Mike and Molly laugh. Molly swooped the little girl up in her arms.

"You look like every fashionable carpenter's helper in New York," Molly declared, giving her a bear hug and a kiss, then setting her back down on the floor. She grinned at Mike. "How about one more cup of coffee before we hit the bricks?"

"Sounds good to me," he agreed.

She motioned him to a chair at the table, then poured them each a cup of coffee and joined him. "I like your hat."

"Oh." He reached up and took it off his head, his grin making his dimple appear. "I'd forgotten I had it until I ran across it yesterday in a box of memorabilia."

"Well, if you're going to remain around these parts, the first thing we need to do is get you a Royals baseball hat. All the kids have them. It's the law—if you're going to live in the Midwest you have to support a Midwest baseball team."

"I'll be sure not to wear my Yankee hat around any of the local law-enforcement officers. I wouldn't want to be arrested and thrown in jail. Unless you're willing to share the cell with me." He placed the hat back on his head.

They smiled at each other and Molly's heart quickened as she felt the electricity that seemed to surge in the air between them. His eyes were the green of nature, deep and earthy, caressing her with the warmth of a summer day. She felt the heat filling her, making her feel light-headed, giddy with a girlish excitement she'd never before experienced.

"More coffee?" she asked, breaking her gaze from his and jumping up from the table.

"No more for me." He stood up. "Are we ready to get this project under way?"

She nodded. "Just let me check one more time on Scotty and I'll be right out."

Mike turned to look at Maggie, who was seated at the kitchen table. "Come on, Maggie. Let's go scope out this job site."

"Just a minute." Maggie jumped down from the kitchen chair and disappeared down the hallway. Mike looked curiously at Molly, but she merely shrugged.

Maggie reappeared seconds later, a bright blue Royals cap on her head at the precise angle Mike's sat on his. "Ready, Freddy." She grinned up at Mike.

Uh-oh, Molly thought. It looks like Maggie is working on a huge case of hero worship. Only five and already she shows excellent taste in men, Molly mused as she watched the two of them disappear into the new room. With a smile twitching at her lips, she went to check on Scotty.

"Hmm, it's going to be a nice-size room," Mike said as he surveyed the shell of the addition. It smelled of freshly cut wood.

"It's gonna be Molly's new bedroom," Maggie said, folding her arms across her chest exactly the way Mike had.

Molly's new bedroom. He was going to help build her new bedroom. It suddenly seemed an intimate thing to do. Her bedroom, the place where she would sleep, dress, and if she were married, it would be in this room where she and her husband would make love. He could easily imagine her in bed, her hair a halo of shimmering gold, her blue eyes radiating desire and love, her body warm and inviting. He knew she would be a wonderful lover, for he knew instinctively that Molly was the type of woman who gave wholly, holding nothing back, hiding no fragments of herself in defense. In that thought was a hint of a warning. She was not a woman to trifle with, no big-city sophisticate who took lovers as regularly as baths. She was a forever kind of woman—and he didn't want to tangle with a forever kind of woman with three kids. He was out here for a year to get his life back together. Who knew where he'd be or what he'd be doing a year from now?

"So, what am I doing here?"

"You're helping Molly build a room."

He didn't realize he had spoken aloud until Maggie answered him, then he grinned. Of course, that's what he was doing, helping her finish a room, being a good neighbor. It was as simple as that. Besides, he and Molly were adults. Surely they could enjoy each other's companionship, perhaps share a kiss or two, without letting their emotions rage out of control.

He turned as Molly came out of the house. "Okay, let's get started," she said brightly. "Maggie, you can go into the kitchen and turn on the television. There are still some cartoons on."

"But I want to help," Maggie protested, her bottom lip pushing out in a pout.

Molly shook her head. "I told you this room is off-limits until it's finished. But, if you're very good this morning, then I'll let you help me fix lunch."

Maggie considered this for a moment, then deciding it pleased her, she nodded and disappeared into the kitchen. Seconds later the sound of cartoons drifted in the air.

"Nice compromise," Mike observed.

Molly grinned. "Compromise is one of the first things you learn when dealing with kids. Now, where do we start?"

"How about in that corner with the plaster-board?"

Molly nodded and together they walked over to the stack of plasterboard. Each grabbed one side of the top piece.

"Was Scotty all right?"

"Fine. He was sleeping."

"That's the best thing for him. Was he born deaf?" Mike asked as they leaned the plasterboard against the wall where they were going to start working.

"No, from what I understand he had a bad case of measles as a baby that resulted in his deafness."

"Hmm, too bad. He seems like a bright kid," Mike said thoughtfully. He positioned the sheet of drywall against the frame. "Now, if you can just lean against this so I can hammer it..." he suggested. Molly nodded and did as he said. Mike grabbed a handful of nails and his hammer. "Now hold it tight," he said, reaching over the top of her to hammer in the first nail. As he pounded, he was aware of the scent of her hair—the clean tangy smell of strawberries. The next nail brought him in contact with the back of her body, and as he felt the rounded curves of her derriere brushing against his thigh, he realized this may be the most wonderfully frustrating job he'd ever done.

"Molly, I've got to go potty," Maggie's voice intruded, bringing him out of his contemplations. "Would you unhook me?"

"Sure, just wait one minute." Molly waited until Mike had banged in several more nails, then she squatted down and grabbed a shoulder strap.

"Damn thing's tricky," Maggie said.

"Maggie, where did you hear that?" Molly asked in surprise.

Mike grinned sheepishly. "I might have mumbled something like that earlier."

"Well, little girls don't say things like that," Molly admonished, unsnapping the overalls.

"Sorry about that," Mike said as Maggie left the room.

"It's all right. Kids have a knack for repeating all the inappropriate words and phrases." They walked back over to grab another sheet of drywall. "I have to admit, I'm glad you're here to help," Molly grunted as they hefted the heavy board into place. "There's no way I could have done this on my own."

"I tried to tell you that," Mike reminded her with a smile.

"Yes, but you didn't strike me as the type of man who would know how to do finish work."

"I'm a man of many hidden talents." There was definitely a note of flirtation in his tone, as if he was personally inviting her to explore his secret hidden talents.

"Sounds fascinating," she murmured. Dear Lord, I'm flirting! she thought in amazement. How many years had it been since she'd indulged in the adult game of flirtatious repartee? She was suddenly reminded that aside from being a mommy, a caretaker of five, she was a woman. It had been a long time since she had acknowledged that fact. She averted her gaze from Mike, afraid of what he might see if he looked into her eyes.

"We're going to need to cut some of this stuff," Mike said, effectively breaking the uncomfortableness of the moment.

For the next few minutes, they worked at setting up sawhorses so that the large sheets could be laid down and cut with the proper tool. "Okay, if you'll hold this right here, I'll cut it."

Molly nodded and leaned over to hold tightly to the edge of the plasterboard as he'd instructed.

He leaned over, the knife in his hand, trying desperately to concentrate on the task of cutting rather than on her. But their faces were inches apart, and her closeness distracted him. He was struck again by her natural beauty. Her skin looked soft and creamy, and he fought the impulse to reach out and run a finger down her cheek. No artificial flavorings or additives, he mused. Just pure all-natural Molly. He laughed out loud at his fanciful thoughts.

"What's so funny?" She smiled, enjoying the sound of his laughter.

"Oh, nothing." His gaze held hers, and instinctively he moved closer, feeling her quickened breath sweetly caressing his face. He wanted to kiss her, and he could tell by the look in her eyes that she wanted him to kiss her.

"What are you guys doing?" Maggie's voice made them both jump.

"We were just getting ready to cut this," Mike said, grabbing the knife tightly in frustration.

Rather than abating, his frustration grew as the day wore on. No matter what they were doing, Maggie seemed to appear between them at the most inappropriate times. And as his frustration grew, his desire for Molly climbed to new heights. He noticed minute details about her that he hadn't noticed before—the light freckles on her forearms, the way she tilted her head when she was listening intently, the way her eyes deepened in hue when she laughed. She was intoxicating, but Maggie was like a police officer, making sure he didn't get drunk and step out of line.

"Thank you," he breathed heavenward when after lunch Molly proclaimed it nap time for Maggie.

And then the ringing of the bell. Scotty had awakened, and with unerring timing rang that infernal bell every time Mike thought he was going to get to spend some time with Molly alone.

The moment Scotty was back asleep, Maggie had awakened from her brief nap.

"It's a conspiracy," Mike muttered with annoyance, swinging the hammer at a nail with more force than necessary.

"I'm here doing hard physical labor to try to win the favor of a woman I don't want to get involved with." He paused a moment, perplexed by this contradiction in thought. Okay, so he desired Molly. She was beautiful and vibrant. But more than that, he had a feeling that in her arms he would find all the ingredients that were missing in his life. He not only desired her, he genuinely liked her. He liked Celia, too, but he'd never felt any sort of physical desire for her. There had been other women he desired, but none with whom he'd found that special combination of emotions he felt for Molly.

What he had to keep reminding himself was that Molly was not a single entity. She came with a ready-made family—a family he didn't want.

He didn't even know why he was stewing about all this now. He really hardly knew Molly, had only shared a single kiss with her. It was a beautiful autumn day, he was enjoying the physical exertion and the company. Why worry about where his feelings for Molly were taking him?

"Just sit back and enjoy the ride."

"Where are we going?" Maggie asked from behind him. The shock of her unexpected voice caused him to miss the nail head he'd been aiming for and bring the hammer squarely down on his thumb. His yelp of pain split the peaceful afternoon, causing Molly to come running from another part of the house.

Mike bit down hard on his lip to trap the string of expletives begging to be released. He was conscious of Maggie's widened eyes looking at him as the pain radiated up his hand and into his arm.

"Are you all right?" Worried lines creased Molly's forehead.

Mike nodded, taking a deep breath. "Maggie surprised me and I missed the nail and connected with my thumb."

"Oh, no, let me see it." Molly took his hand in hers. Her touch was achingly tender as she perused the thumb with the expertise of a mother accustomed to dealing with youthful smashed fingers.

Molly's emotions as she held Mike's hand were less than maternal, however. His thumb was already turning a bright purple beneath the nail, but she hardly noticed this fact. What she did notice was the masculine smell of him, the clean tang of honest sweat mingling with the subtle scent of a spicy cologne applied earlier in the day. His hand was large, with long delicate fingers. They would be capable of strength, but equally capable of gentleness and comfort. She felt a warmth invade her body as she wondered what they would feel like splayed against her naked flesh. She released his hand quickly, wondering what it was about this man that caused even the most innocent bodily contact to become something invitingly erotic in her mind.

"You may lose your thumbnail," she said softly.

"Maybe," he agreed.

"Molly has to kiss it," Maggie stated emphatically.

"Oh, I don't think that's necessary," Molly demurred.

"Yes, it is. You always say kisses are the best medicine."

"Oh, she does?" Mike's eyes sparked in amusement. "Well, who am I to argue with Molly?" He held out his hand. "Molly, kiss my boo-boo."

It's only a game, Mike thought—for Maggie's benefit. But as Molly took his hand and pressed her lips gently against his injured thumb, his eyes looked deeply into hers as he realized it was not a game at all. She was beginning to care for him—it was there on her face for him to see.

Suddenly he was afraid. Their attraction to each other was spinning out of control, and he knew he was going to have to be the one to regain his equilibrium and pull them out of the spin that was heading them straight for disaster. He had wanted only a little light romance with her. But somehow their feelings had already surpassed that level. She had three children and he couldn't stand the thought of being around kids, having them depend on him. He'd had enough of that, and he'd failed miserably. Any further relationship between them could only end with one of them sporting a major heartache.

"I think it's time to call it a day," he said, pulling his hand gently from her grasp.

"It's early yet. I was thinking maybe you'd stay for supper."

"I don't think it's possible," he answered, and she had a feeling he wasn't talking only about dinner. He picked up his hammer and hung it back on his belt. "I'll see you later."

"Wait," Maggie commanded, scurrying over to him. "I didn't give you my kiss. Two kisses will make your boo-boo get better really fast." She grabbed his hand and planted a slightly slobbery kiss on his thumb. "There, now my grouch will feel all better." She smiled widely.

As Mike looked down at her, he remembered another child who had looked at him with trusting eyes. He turned abruptly and walked away.

"Will he be back tomorrow?" Maggie asked, coming to stand next to Molly.

Molly stared at Mike's retreating figure, seeing the rigid set of his shoulders as he slowly walked away. Something had happened to cause him to withdraw emotionally, as well as physically. "I don't know, Maggie," she answered thoughtfully. "I really don't know."

Chapter Seven

Molly sat curled up on the sofa, her gaze focused blankly on the television set, but her thoughts were far away from the late-evening sitcom rerun.

Mike—she'd been thinking about him ever since he'd left so abruptly that afternoon. He'd been flirtatious and fun for most of the day and they had worked well together, completing much of the drywalling.

She had been surprised at the depth of her disappointment when he'd left so suddenly. She'd been hoping he would stay for supper, spend some time with her kids, get to know them individually. She knew that the thought of three children could be overwhelming, but if he'd just give them a chance, he would see they were wonderful human beings.

She jumped as the telephone rang and she scurried to answer it before it woke the children.

"Molly, it's Mike."

"I was just thinking about you," she said.

"Good thoughts, I hope."

There is was again, the flirting lilt that had an undeniable pull on her. She thought of the strangeness of his gaze when she had kissed his thumb. It was almost as if he pulled her close for the sole purpose of pushing her away.

"They were good thoughts," she answered slowly. "I was disappointed that you didn't stay for dinner."

"That's part of the reason I'm calling—to explain my sudden departure." There was a long pause and then he continued, "Molly, I think it's pretty obvious something is going on between us. I feel it and you feel it, and it's ridiculous for us to pretend it doesn't exist. I'm very attracted to you, and I think you are to me, too."

Molly felt a warm blush steal over her at the stark openness of his words. She was also pleased by what he was saying. "I am," she agreed in a soft voice.

"I left your house today with the idea that I wouldn't be back tomorrow, that I didn't want to see you anymore. But I do."

Her heart leapt at his admission, but her joy was short-lived as he continued, "However, there is a problem."

"What?"

There was another long silence. "I want to see you, but I don't want to give you any false ideas or hopes concerning future commitments. Molly, I don't like kids," he finished flatly.

Her first reaction was to protest. She'd seen him with Scotty and Maggie earlier, and his demeanor had not been that of a man who didn't like kids. In fact, she had been encouraged by what she perceived as his natural affinity with children. No, she refused to believe that Mike didn't like kids, but she also couldn't protest and deny him what he thought he felt. She sensed that for some reason it was important to him to cling to his belief that he didn't like children.

"So, where do we go from here?" Her guard was up. *Surely he isn't going to ask me to get rid of the kids,* she thought. *I've been through that particular heartache before, with David. If Mike makes me choose, then he isn't the kind of man I want in my life.* She realized she was holding her breath while awaiting his answer.

"Molly, I wouldn't ask you to stop foster parenting," he said as if able to read her mind. "All I want is to keep seeing you, enjoying your company, without being guilty of leading you on. You realize I'm only here in Parsons for a year."

"Okay," she agreed, but not without a certain tinge of disappointment licking deep within her. "No strings attached," she added, realizing she was willing to take it one day at a time.

"Great," he replied, as if an enormous weight had been lifted from his shoulders. "Well look, I'll be there tomorrow as soon as the kids leave for school."

"Okay, I'll see you in the morning." Molly hung up, a warmth invading her as effectively as if she was sitting in front of a roaring open fire.

He liked her. He wanted to go on seeing her. He liked being with her. But then the warmth seeped away somewhat as she recalled her own words. *No strings attached.* Throughout her life those words had marked her relationships with other people. As a foster parent, she was accustomed to love with no strings.

"But he doesn't hate kids," she said aloud. She knew in her heart that Mike Wakefield couldn't hate children, no matter how he protested otherwise.

"Molly Smith, you wicked woman," she admonished herself with a devilish grin. "You didn't even mention to him that the kids don't have school tomorrow." With a small smile still curving her lips, she shut off the television and went to bed.

"Carrie, Wendy, there is a box of sandpaper in the kitchen. Why don't you each run in and grab a couple of sheets," Mike instructed, pausing to wipe his forehead with the back of one hand. He tried to ignore Maggie standing at his side, imitating his actions with the accuracy of a miniature shadow.

He'd tried to ignore all the kids when he'd first arrived earlier in the day. But Molly's kids were as difficult to ignore as a blizzard in July.

When he'd discovered they were out of school due to a teachers' meeting, his initial impulse had been to bail out, turn tail and run. It had been the silent challenge in Molly's eyes that had stiffened his backbone and made him decide to stay.

Actually it hadn't been as bad as he had expected. During the morning hours, the kids had watched television, their cooperation allowing Mike and Molly to finish putting up the drywall and doing the plastering. Lunch was peanut-butter-and-jelly sandwiches, and by the time they were finished eating, the joint compound on the walls was dry enough to sand. It was then Molly decided to let the kids help.

Jimmy and Scotty, who was over his bout with the flu, were eager to help, as were Molly's baby-sitting charges, Wendy and Carrie. Mike handed them each a piece of sandpaper and put them all to work.

Within minutes, each child was working on a different wall. They created clouds of dust as they moved their sandpaper back and forth. Maggie was like a little butterfly, flitting from child to child, but always drawn back to Mike as if he were a particularly colorful flower.

"No, Scotty, go in the same direction." Mike jumped up and showed the boy what he meant. "If you go in too many directions with the sandpaper you make ridges." Scotty frowned, not understanding what Mike was trying to tell him. Mike heard Molly's throaty chuckle from behind him. She quickly signed to Scotty, who nodded in understanding, grinned at Mike, then turned back to his task.

"I think I need a course in remedial sign language," he said, as he and Molly sat down on a sawhorse in the center of the room. "You seem to do it so effortlessly. Did you have to learn it when the boys were placed with you?''

"I first learned it in college. I majored in elementary education, with emphasis on children with special needs. The agency learned that I knew sign language and immediately placed Scotty and Jimmy in my care.'' She smiled. "It's not difficult. I'd be happy to teach it to you sometime.''

His eyes warmed with renewed admiration. "What made you decide to become a foster parent?''

"It's a long story. I'll tell you all about it sometime.''

"I'll hold you to it.'' His gaze drank her in. "I want to know everything there is to know about you.'' He was surprised to find this was true. Oh, he knew how the sunlight loved her hair, and he knew how the sound of her laugh made his blood thicken. He knew how easily she expressed affection to the children, but he wanted to know all her secrets, her past, all the things that made up the essence of her.

His eyes held hers in a gaze that was almost hypnotic as he tried to communicate all these things to her.

He took in the picture of her in the jeans that hugged her hips, the T-shirt that managed to look as sexy as any fitted designer gown he'd ever seen on a woman. Molly was just right—all rounded curves and the promise of warmth. Just right for snuggling with in front of a fire. Just right for making love with on a cold wintry morning, or in the middle of a field with the summer sun on their bodies.

Although he said none of this aloud, he realized the direction of his thoughts must be apparent on his face, for she blushed hotly and turned away, mumbling something about being thirsty. He grinned widely, watching her go, wondering if she had any idea that her back view was just as enticing as her front. Her derriere had just enough wiggle to give a man wicked thoughts.

Molly walked into the kitchen and straight to the sink, where she got herself a glass of cold water. She took a long sip, then rubbed the cool glass across her forehead and sighed. The day was warmer than usual, but she knew her overheating had nothing to do with the heat of the sun. It was Mike, with his unspoken words and taunting eyes that was causing an inferno to rage inside her. She felt like a nuclear reactor that had reached meltdown, a volcano with lava that was about to spew. Without touching her, he was causing her to feel things no man had every made her feel before. He wanted her. His eyes spoke that fact more eloquently than his lips could ever do. And that knowledge caused both exhilaration and fear.

She listened to his voice drifting from the other room, directing the kids' activities as effortlessly as a field marshall overseeing his troops. She smiled, hearing Maggie's delighted giggles. Her smile slowly faded, being replaced by a thoughtful frown. Why did he continue to profess to dislike children when it was so obviously not true?

She'd been a little worried about how he would react when he arrived that morning to find a whole crew awaiting him. His eyes had darkened with shadowed pain, reflecting his initial impulse to run, and she'd wondered if she'd made a major mistake, scared him away for good. But he'd merely whispered that she would pay later, then walked into the new room, the kids all trailing behind him as if he were the Pied Piper.

She smiled again, thinking of his words of warning. There had been a glow in his eyes when he'd murmured them, a glow that had made her feel that somehow she wouldn't mind paying the price he requested. She took another long drink of the cold water, envisioning steam blowing out of her ears as the cold water made contact with her molten thoughts.

"Molly, Mike said for me to come and get you," Carrie announced from behind her, her dark eyes sparking with excitement. "Mike says we're all going to play hide-and-seek. Come on, Molly." She grabbed Molly's hand and tugged impatiently.

"All right, all right, I'm coming." She laughed at Carrie's excitement.

"What's this I hear about a game of hide-and-seek?" Molly asked as she found Mike and the rest of the kids in the front yard.

"Even though it's early in the day, I thought we all deserved a break," Mike explained. "I thought the kids might enjoy a game of hide-and-seek." His words were met with an enthusiastic cheer from the children. He held up his hands to quiet them. "Only my game of hide-and-seek is a little bit different."

"Different how?" Molly asked.

"In my game, the kids all shut their eyes, and you and I go hide."

She felt the familiar warmth begin to invade her body as she saw the languid look of desire in his eyes. "Okay," he continued, talking to the kids. "You all turn around and hide your eyes and count to one hundred and Molly and I will go hide. Then, you come and find us." He waited until Molly finished signing to Scott and Jimmy, then he grabbed her hand and pulled her away. "And no peeking," he commanded over his shoulder.

"Where are we going?" she asked breathlessly as he pulled her around the back of the barn.

"In here," he instructed, pointing to a small window in the wall of the barn.

"You've got to be kidding." She laughed. "Why didn't we just go in the front way if you wanted to hide in here?"

"The kids would have seen us going in. Come on, I'll give you a leg up." He boosted her up and through the window, chuckling as he heard her hit the hay on the other side. He was through the window in a flash, joining her on the soft bed of hay.

She immediately sat up, feeling almost oppressed by the darkness of the barn, the silence surrounding them, the overwhelming nearness of him.

"Molly..." he breathed, as he sat up next to her, so close her mouth went dry in anticipation.

She turned her head to look at him, gasping as his lips firmly claimed hers. This kiss had absolutely nothing in common with the light one they had shared on the night of the dance. This one was intense, breath-stealing, and as it lingered, she felt as if not only their lips were touching, but their very souls were melding.

"I've wanted to do that all day," he sighed as he broke the kiss momentarily.

"Hmm, you should have done it earlier," she answered softly, leaning against him, enjoying the strength in his broad shoulders, the rock-hard planes of his physique.

"Why is that?"

"Because you do it so well," she murmured.

Her words lit a fire deep within him, and with a moan, he reclaimed her lips. His hands went to her waist, urging her closer as his mouth drank deeply from hers. Molly followed his lead, winding her arms around his neck, molding her upper body against his. She loved the taste of him, the feel of him, the scent of him—and the realization struck her with a suddenness that stole her breath. She was on the verge of falling in love with Mike Wakefield.

"Hi, guys."

They sprang apart as Maggie appeared before them as if by magic. "I found them," she yelled toward the barn door. "They're in the barn. And they were kissing."

"This is my favorite time of the day," Molly said as she and Mike sat down on the porch swing. She pulled her sweater more tightly around her neck. "When the kids are in bed and the house is quiet, and we've all made it through another day without any major catastrophes."

Mike put his arm around her, pulling her closer against his side. "I have a feeling that you handle catastrophes exceedingly well."

"You learn quickly with three children depending on you."

"You promised you'd tell me how you got started foster parenting," he reminded her, his hand lightly playing with the ends of her hair. She was conscious of the press of his thigh against hers, the feel of his hand caressing her hair and neck. He was making it difficult for her to think about anything but the kisses they had shared earlier, the way his breath had warmed her face, her neck. She moved away from him slightly, needing space to think about his question.

"What's wrong?" he asked, instantly missing the warmth of her pressed against him.

"I can't think when you're so close to me," she answered.

"Good." He grinned at her, then sobered, removing his arm from around her. "Okay, let's talk, then we'll cuddle."

His grin was infectious, and she found herself responding in kind. "Tell me about your foster parenting," he prompted again, and this time his tone told her he was ready for a more serious discussion.

She stared off into the distance of the night. "I was five years old when I was placed here on the farm as a foster child. The Smiths, Walter and Margaret, were wonderful people. They not only fed me and clothed me, they taught me all about love. When I was ten, they adopted me, and when I was in high school, they began taking in other foster children.'' She smiled reflectively, remembering all the years of love she'd had here on the farm with the Smiths. "You know, with them, there was always room for one more, always more than enough love to go around."

"What happened to them?" Mike asked, his arm going around her once again, as if anticipating a tragedy.

"Eight years ago they were driving home from a city-council meeting and a driver in an oncoming car fell asleep at the wheel and hit them head-on. They died instantly.''

She hadn't even been aware of his arm around her until he tightened his grasp on her shoulder, as if the warmth of his embrace could shelter her from the coldness of painful memories.

"I had just graduated from college, wasn't sure where I was going with my life. Suddenly, I was left with a farm and two foster kids who had nowhere to go. That was the beginning.''

"Isn't it unusual for a single person to be a foster parent?''

Molly shook her head. "Not so much anymore. There's such a need for good foster care. So many children needing love and attention. The restrictions are ever changing to accommodate increasing numbers of homeless children.'' She smiled apologetically. "Don't get me started talking about foster care—I immediately climb up on my soapbox.''

"How do you do it? I mean, financially, isn't it difficult to be raising three children?"

She shrugged. "We make do. Of course there's my baby-sitting, and I sell an occasional quilt. We also sell fruits and vegetables in the spring and summer, and chicken eggs all year round. I've got forty acres that are worked by a friend and we share the profits." She smiled. "I guess when something is important enough, you find ways to make it work. And these kids are important."

Mike was silent, staring off into the darkness as if the night held something fascinating. Again Molly saw the darkness of shadows in his eyes, but she said nothing, afraid to intrude.

Mike was lost in time, remembering how it had once been for him. There had been a time when he'd burned with commitment, when the most important thing in his life had been taking care of sick children, helping them heal. He'd been damn good at it, too. The kids had trusted him and the parents had adored him. Success had come easy, both financially and professionally. Then, little things had begun to color his perspective. Finally, the straw that had broken his spirit—he'd lost a patient. He winced painfully at the memory. "Molly, I'm a pediatrician."

Her eyes widened in surprise. "A pediatrician? But I don't understand. The way you feel about children . . ."

"Oh, Molly—" Mike sighed "—I don't hate kids. I couldn't hate them and choose to be a pediatrician. I took a leave of absence from my practice and decided to come out here for a while because things were going badly for me." He shifted on the seat, causing it to swing rhythmically back and forth. "When I first became a doctor, I loved my work and my patients. It was a constant struggle to pay the office rent, and many of my patients' families couldn't afford high medical bills. But every day was a challenge, and I felt good about what I was accomplishing. Then I met Celia and things began to change."

"Who's Celia?" Molly asked, trying to sound nonchalant, but feeling a sudden jealousy raising its head.

He laughed. "Celia is the most neurotic wealthy young woman in New York. She was raised with money, divorced money, and now divides her time between visiting her therapist and shopping. But about three years ago when I met her, she decided to sponsor me, introduce me to the prominent of the city. She talked me into changing the location of my office, and suddenly I found my patient list reading like a who's who of the rich and famous."

"And it was then things started to go bad?" Molly wasn't sure she understood the connection.

He shook his head. "Not right away, but over the past six months, things started bothering me in a way they never had before. The kids were getting on my nerves. The kids' parents were getting on my nerves."

"Sounds like a bad case of burnout," she said.

He nodded. "It began as that." Again he sought the darkness of the night with his eyes, retreating from Molly as he climbed into his memory. "I had this patient, a cute little kid named Billy. I first saw him when his mother brought him in for his six-month checkup. Six months old, bald head and all eyes—the kid was something special." His smile was suddenly warm. "I saw him pretty often when he was a baby, lots of childhood complaints, but nothing serious. He was my buddy. As he got older he'd climb up on the table and say, 'I love Doc Mike.'" He winced as if the memories were physically painful. "Anyway, he was six when his mother brought him in and I diagnosed him with leukemia." Molly placed a hand on his arm, wanting to help him through this, share it with him to ease his burden. "I turned him over to a cancer specialist, and I honestly believed we'd be able to cure him. We couldn't. He died . . . and that's when I decided no more doctoring, no more kids."

"Oh, Mike, I'm so sorry."

He shrugged. "It's over and done with." His eyes shuttered darkly, letting her know the subject was closed. "We did good work today." He moved his feet to rock the swing once again. "A little more sanding on the wall joints and we should be able to paint."

"Oh, it's going to be wonderful to have a nice big bedroom where I can not only sleep, but actually walk all around the sides of the bed. The room I use now is so small I can barely walk around the furniture."

"There are other interesting things that can take place in a bedroom besides sleeping and walking around the furniture," he said. He took one hand and trailed it slowly from her earlobe down the length of her jaw, one finger pausing to rub sensually over her lips. "Those kisses in the barn this afternoon only whetted my appetite. While I sat across from you at the dinner table, I wanted to grab the fork out of your hand and throw you down on the table and make love to you then and there."

Molly wanted to giggle at the image that instantly sprang to mind, that of Mike throwing her down on the table and her head coming to rest in the huge bowl of mashed potatoes. But the giggle never made it to her lips as, instead, his mouth covered hers, the warmth filling every part of her, chasing frivolity far away. His tongue immediately sought hers, touching tentatively, then when welcomed, thrusting teasingly with her own.

She turned on the swing seat, wanting to be enveloped by him, needing to feel him pressed tightly against her. Her hands sought the back of his neck, lightly caressing the dark hair on the nape. Mike uttered a lover's sigh against her mouth as she molded herself into him, pressing her breasts against his firmly muscled chest. His hands crept up under her sweater and T-shirt, caressing her back with the lightness of butterfly wings against the petal of a flower, evoking a moan of pleasure from her.

Still their lips clung together, as if sharing breath while underwater, and in truth, Molly felt as if she had suddenly been plunged beneath the surface of a deep lake. She was drowning in sensation, giving in to the languor that beckoned her. As his hands wandered around to lightly graze the top of her lacy bra, she instinctively arched against him, wanting more than his featherlight caresses, wanting—

"Molly, I had a bad dream."

They jumped apart like guilty teenagers being confronted by an angry parent. Maggie stood in the front doorway, rubbing her eyes, a blanket clutched in her hand.

"Come on, Bean." Molly gestured for Maggie to join them. She wrapped the blanket around the little girl, then swooped her up in her arms. Maggie immediately snuggled into the warmth of Molly's embrace and closed her eyes.

Molly looked at Mike, knowing her eyes were filled with apology and regret. "I'm sorry," she said, feeling her face flaming.

"It's all right," he answered, kicking his feet slightly so the swing began to move softly back and forth once again. "But I think it's only fair that I tell you I lied."

She smoothed a strand of Maggie's hair, then looked at him curiously. "What did you lie about?"

"I really do hate kids." But there was a gentle smile on his face that belied his words. He put his arm around her shoulder and pulled her close. She rested her head on his shoulder, feeling a rightness she had never known before. He must have felt it, too, because for a very long time he held her close, keeping the swing moving gently to and fro.

Chapter Eight

"I don't believe this." Mike smiled at Molly across the table in Wanda's Café. "I can't believe we actually shared a meal where there were no fights, no interruptions, no prepubescent voices to fill the natural silences."

"It was nice, wasn't it," Molly agreed, pushing her empty plate away and sighing with contentment.

Contentment—she'd been feeling a lot of that lately. For the first time in her life she felt whole, complete, and she knew it had everything to do with the man sitting across from her. She hadn't realized there was a hole in her heart until he stepped into her life to fill it.

"We're going to have to buy Leslie an extra-special present to thank her for giving us this night to celebrate the completion of your room." His gaze was as warm as a caress.

She blushed with pleasure, wondering if he was aware of the habit he'd fallen into, the habit of using the word "we" instead of the singular. "We need to buy a present." He'd been doing that a lot lately. "We should see about getting the kids a computer for Christmas." "We need to get Jimmy's eyes checked, I think he may need glasses."

The children had easily accepted Mike into their lives. Often, in the evenings after supper, it was Mike who helped the kids with their homework while Molly cleaned up the supper dishes. And later, when the kids were all in bed, if Maggie awoke and needed some reassurance, she was just as apt to crawl up into his lap as Molly's.

Yet, no matter how well he had melded into her family structure, no matter how much she was finding herself drawn to him, she was aware of the fact that their relationship was following the terms he had dictated. No strings, no commitments, no talk of happily-ever-after. He was here for a year, recovering from a painful episode that had shaken him badly. And he was healing, she'd seen signs of his progress every day for the past two weeks as they'd finished her new bedroom. She had learned to accept each day with him as a gift, content to take what he offered and savoring the moments they had together.

"It's still early. What do you say we get out of here, go back to my place where we can celebrate the completion of the room addition with a glass of wine and

maybe a little necking." He grinned, watching the
blush that crept up her neck to color her cheeks. He
loved to make her blush, found it a charming feminine trait he'd forgotten existed.

"That sounds nice," she murmured.

"What, the wine or the necking?" he teased,
watching her blush deepened.

"Both," she admitted with a small smile, her gaze
boldly meeting his. Both of them knew what would
happen if they went back to his place. He knew they
would make love, and as he looked in her eyes and realized she knew it, heat infused him.

They'd had precious little time alone, having to
make do with furtive kisses stolen behind the barn,
quick caresses in the hallway. And always, there was
the passion-stilting presence of children nearby. But
tonight, the evening stretched before them. Leslie was
sitting with the kids and he and Molly were two con-
senting adults.

Suddenly he couldn't wait to get her out of this
public restaurant and back to his house where they
could be truly alone.

"Ready?" He looked at her expectantly. She nodded and together they got up from the table.

She looks so beautiful tonight, he thought, his gaze
lingering on her while he waited his turn at the cashier. Her hair was softly curling around her face and a
touch of mascara enhanced the blueness of her eyes.
The peach-colored sweater dress she was wearing was
V-necked, giving him a tantalizing hint of the full
breasts beneath. Never, in the month that he had

known her, had she looked so desirable, so achingly touchable. His mouth grew dry as he anticipated the night yet to come.

"Sir?"

He flushed, realizing the cashier was waiting for him. He fumbled with his wallet, finding himself clumsy. *My God, I'm nervous,* he thought in amazement. He felt the same kind of intense nervousness that he'd felt when he'd been a teenager and had bought a condom and gone over to the house of a girl who had a reputation for being wild. She hadn't been home, and he'd been relieved because in truth he hadn't been sure how to use the thing in the little foil packet and he'd been afraid he would do something wrong and she would laugh at him. Now he was feeling that same kind of anxiety, afraid that somehow he would do something wrong and ruin things between him and Molly. Get yourself under control, he mentally commanded, realizing his palms were sweating.

"All set," he said, joining her at the door. He paused, seeing her frown. "Anything wrong?"

"No, I was just wondering if maybe I should call home and make sure everything is all right." She looked over at the pay phone on the wall, then at him. "No—" she smiled ruefully "—I'm being ridiculous. I'm sure everything is fine. Let's go." She linked her arm through his, and as they stepped out of the restaurant she lay her head against his shoulder and smiled up at him. In that instant, his nervousness vanished. He knew with a certainty that everything was going to be fine.

They drove to his house in silence, not needing words to fill the quiet. The car heater blew warm air, providing them an isolated cocoon against the cold night. She hadn't been to his house since that morning weeks earlier when he had stepped on the apple pie. At that time none of his furniture had arrived yet. Now he found himself anxious to see what she would think of his home. Although it was funny, really—he'd begun to think of Molly's place as home, much more so than his own lonely house.

"Come in and make yourself comfortable. I'll get the wine and make a fire," he said when they'd arrived and he had led her into the living room.

She nodded, looking around with interest. Mike went into the kitchen to grab a bottle of wine and two glasses. He returned to find her studying an abstract painting hanging on one of the walls. "It's titled *Chaos*. It was painted by a friend of mine, a doctor back in New York." He set the wine and goblets on the glass-topped coffee table, then lit a match and touched it to the paper and kindling beneath the already laid fire in the fireplace.

"It's interesting," she murmured.

"Actually, it's awful, just like the furniture in this room," he said, rising as the fire began to flame.

"It's not awful," she protested with a small smile. "It all looks like it belongs in an ultramodern glass-and-steel town house."

"It did." He laughed. "But it doesn't belong here, with the rich woods and carved moldings. High-tech furniture for the high-tech man I used to be. Why don't we sit down here in front of the fire?'' He motioned to the black-and-rose Oriental rug that lay in front of the hearth. Molly sat down, taking the glass of wine he offered her. He turned off the light that had been on when they'd arrived and joined her on the rug.

She'd looked beautiful before, in the artificial glare of the restaurant lights, but she looked positively breathtaking with the firelight playing on her hair and skin.

"You're staring," she said, taking a sip of her wine.

"I know." He stretched out full-length on his side next to her. He reached up and touched a strand of her hair that was shimmering as if filled with the light of a hundred fireflies. "I can't help myself. You look so beautiful."

"You're just trying to seduce me with smooth flattery," she laughed, taking another sip of her wine.

"Is is working?"

She pretended to think. "I'm not quite sure. Flatter me some more."

The hand that had been lightly caressing her hair slowly moved up her neck and across her cheek. His finger grazed her cheekbone, moving sensually back and forth across her skin. "The fire makes your skin look like rich honey," he murmured. A small smile touched his lips. "And I love the taste of honey."

"Hmm, it's definitely working," she said breathlessly, his words and his gentle touch causing a languid heat to steal over her body.

"We should let Leslie stay with the kids more often," he whispered, taking her wineglass from her and setting it on the coffee table.

At his mention of the children, Molly felt a dark shadow sweep over her. It was the same kind of foreboding that had encompassed her while she had been waiting for him to pay the tab in the restaurant. It was nothing deeply profound or earth-shattering, more like a prickly scalp or an itchy palm.

"Molly, is something wrong?" He looked at her intently, making her realize her uneasiness had been communicated to him.

"I definitely need to get away more often," she said, consciously pushing her disquietude aside. "Get me away from the kids and I don't even know how to act."

"I'll be happy to show you how to act," he replied, and the flame Molly saw in his eyes had nothing to do with a reflection from the fireplace.

His lips met hers, his tongue immediately teasing and exploring. As he kissed her, he gently maneuvered her so that she was laying down next to him. Their bodies melded together, chest to breasts, hips to hips. It felt right, they fit perfectly, as if they were interlocking pieces of a jigsaw puzzle. His mouth left hers, moving across her cheek to nibble on her earlobe.

Molly moved her arms around his back, reveling in the feel of his firm muscles moving just beneath the material of his shirt. She wanted to feel his skin, have its warmth and vitality right beneath her fingertips.

She tugged impatiently at his shirt. Sensing her desire, he sat up, unbuttoned his shirt and took it off, exposing his torso to her gaze and touch.

He returned to her embrace and she renewed her tactile scrutiny of the flat planes and sculptured muscles of his back. His skin was warm, and so alive beneath her fingers. Yet as good as he felt, as right as she felt in his arm, she couldn't shake the strange apprehension that had followed her throughout the evening, like a shadow that refused to be banished. She found it impossible to surrender completely to the mindless pleasure his caresses provoked.

You're just not used to being away from the kids, she told herself, catching her breath as his hand wandered between them to gently cup one of her breasts. She wanted to relinquish herself to this moment with this man. She wanted to succumb to the fire he was stoking in her. She craved the abandonment he offered, the joy of giving and receiving love.

But something is wrong at home, an inner voice protested.

"Molly? Is something wrong?" He pulled slightly away from her and studied her.

"No, everything's fine."

He smiled down at her and brushed a strand of hair from her face. "You know, there is nothing I would like more than to make love to you. But when I do, I want it to be when you are free to give me all of yourself—and I don't think it's going to happen at this moment." He touched the tip of her nose. "Call home. Make sure everything is all right."

Molly expelled a sigh, amazed at the depth of his perception. "I really do feel like a fool," she said as he reached up to the coffee table and brought the phone down to her. "I'm sure everything's fine, but I just keep getting this terrible foreboding." She smiled ruefully. "You probably think I'm being ridiculous."

"On the contrary, I've been a doctor far too long to dismiss mother's intuition."

She smiled gratefully and punched in her home phone number. Her smile slowly faded as the phone rang three . . . four . . . five times. "Nobody's answering." She clutched the phone more tightly against her ear.

Mike heard the anxiety in her voice and quickly grabbed his shirt from the floor.

"Leslie," she breathed into the phone in relief. Mike relaxed. "What? When did it start? We'll be right home." Molly hung up the phone and looked up at Mike, her face pale. "Leslie said Maggie is coughing and can't seem to catch her breath."

Mike pulled on his shirt and helped Molly to her feet.

"Mike, I'm sorry."

He pulled her against him for a moment and kissed her quickly on the forehead. "Come on, let's got see what's wrong with our little Magpie."

It took them only minutes to get to Molly's house, where they found Leslie holding a frightened coughing Maggie. Scotty and Jimmy stood nearby, their faces white with anxiety.

"Oh, thank God you're here!" Leslie exclaimed, grateful to relinquish the child into Mike's awaiting arms. "She started getting hoarse just before dinner, then began coughing, and I couldn't get her to stop."

"It's croup," Mike diagnosed immediately, recognizing the familiar harsh barking cough. "Molly, go start the hot water in the shower. Make the bathroom fill with steam. Leslie, why don't you reassure the other kids and get them into bed." The commands came easily, his doctor persona firmly in place. He then turned his attention to the child in his arms. "Hey, Magpie, don't be scared. We're going to fix you right up." He kept his voice even and modulated, not wanting to scare the little girl any more than she already was. Her face was strained and her natural color was gone, the exertion of pulling for each breath leaving her pale. "Now, what we're going to do is take you into the bathroom. It will be easier for you to breathe in there." He carried her into the steam-filled room, where Molly was waiting for them.

"Here, I'll take her." Molly sat down on the stool and took Maggie in her arms, relieved to hear some of the child's breathing distress lessening. She smoothed Maggie's damp hair from her face, rocking her back and forth in the time-honored instinct of mothers everywhere.

Mike leaned against the sink, watching them through the swirling steam, understanding Molly's need to hold Maggie, impart the love that was as important to the healing process as any medicine.

Within minutes, Maggie's breathing had eased enough to allow her to fall asleep, exhausted by the physical trauma.

"I've often fantasized taking a steamy hot shower with you, but this isn't exactly the scenario I envisioned," Mike said softly, knowing the immediate crisis had passed.

Molly smiled, looking ethereal in the misty steam. "This isn't exactly my idea of a hot date, either." Her smile faded and she looked down at Maggie, worry once again lining her face. "Is she going to be all right?"

"She'll be fine," he assured her. "In the morning I'll write you out a prescription for an antibiotic, just in case she's fighting off some sort of infection."

"It scared the daylights out of me."

He nodded. "She'll be exhausted. It's sort of like trying to sip a soda through a bent straw."

She studied Maggie's sleeping countenance. "I don't know what I'd do without her."

He looked at the two of them, seeing something pure and beautiful in Molly's love, the unquestioning commitment to the child. There was no holding back, no defenses intact. "What's Maggie's story?" he asked, curious about the little girl's background.

"There's not much story to tell. From what Social Services has told me, Maggie was found abandoned in a motel room in Wichita, Kansas. She was two, and the agency thought she'd been left there alone for at least a couple of days." She gripped Maggie closer to her and her face tensed with anger. "It enrages me every time I think about it—this poor child, hungry, alone and frightened.'' She relaxed somewhat, the anger gone as quickly as it had appeared. ''Maggie has no memory of that, thank God. But on a subconscious level it's there with her, emotional baggage she'll probably carry with her for the rest of her life.'' She smoothed Maggie's hair once again. ''It's what makes her awaken sometimes in the middle of the night, needing to know that somebody's there for her.''

''We all have the need to know somebody's there when we wake up in the middle of the night,'' he said. He straightened up and cleared his voice, as if embarrassed by his words. ''Keep her in here another ten minutes or so, and I'll go check on Leslie and the two boys.'' He opened the door, disappearing into the hall along with a cloud of steam.

Molly plucked at her dress, which had become damp and uncomfortable, and shifted Maggie to a more relaxed position in her arms. She looked down at the little girl, but her thoughts were on the man who had just left the room.

She knew he had been disappointed by the fact that their evening hadn't gone as planned. So was she. But no matter how wonderfully he would have made love to her, no matter what expertise he would have shown in the act of physically joining, nothing could have affected her as much as his selfless act of denial in calling a halt to their lovemaking. He could have forced the issue, ignoring the feeling of unease she had. But instead he had honored her feelings, and in not making love to her he had made her realize how much she had come to care for him.

She wasn't surprised to realize she cared about him. How could she not? He was a gentle man with a wonderful sense of humor and kisses that made her forget a lifetime of loneliness. She thought of what she knew of his life back in New York. What little bit she'd learned was troubling; it felt threatening. Art galleries, charity affairs, the opera—a far cry from what Parsons, Kansas, had to offer. She was afraid that somehow New York would hunt him down, seduce him with its erratic pulse and abandoned ways, drawing him back there as effectively as sea sirens of myth once pulled sailors to their deaths. But of course he would go back, she reminded herself. He'd made it clear from the very beginning that he was here in Parsons only temporarily.

"Molly, I'm all wet," Maggie murmured, stirring in Molly's arms.

"Okay, Bean. We'll get you out of here and into some nice dry pajamas." She sat Maggie on the floor and reached over and turned off the hot water. She was grateful for any task that kept her mind off her troubling thoughts of Mike and what the future held for them.

Not only did she put Maggie in fresh pajamas, she also changed her own steam-dampened dress, exchanging it for a comfortable jogging suit. She then carried Maggie into the living room and lay her on the sofa, where the child immediately fell into a restless sleep.

"Where's everyone else?" she asked Mike as he walked into the living room from the kitchen.

"I sent Leslie home and the two boys are in bed. Come on in here and sit down. I made a fresh pot of coffee and even managed to find a box of animal crackers in one of your cabinets."

"But what about . . . ?" She looked back at Maggie, lines of worry furrowing her brow.

"She'll be fine," he assured her, taking her by the shoulders and leading her into the kitchen. "What Maggie needs most is sleep, and if she has another coughing spell we can hear her from here." He gave Molly a gentle push into a chair at the table. She murmured her thanks as he handed her a steaming mug of fresh coffee and set a bowl of animal crackers in front of her.

"You mean Maggie might have another spell?" she asked after taking a sip of the hot brew.

"It's possible." He joined her at the table, noting the concern that still darkened her eyes. "But it's been my experience that any crisis can be overcome with a cup of coffee and a handful of animal crackers."

Her eyes lightened somewhat. "What do you know about the pleasures of animal crackers?"

He shrugged and plucked a lion-shaped cracker out of the bowl. "I know that lions are the best."

She laughed. "Not true. They're all the same flavor."

"Impossible. The lions are definitely better."

As she watched, he carefully lined up several of the cookies on the table in front of him, each of them a

different animal shape. She grinned in amusement as
he proceeded to conduct an impromptu taste test.
"Definitely the lions are the best," he proclaimed after having tasted each one. He grinned, making his
provocative dimple appear. "But I have to admit, part
of it might be a psychological thing. There's something very appealing to one's machismo about biting
off the head of a vicious lion."

She lifted one of her pale eyebrows, knowing perfectly well what he was doing—entertaining her with
inane conversation in an effort to take her mind of
Maggie. And for just a moment, it had worked.
"Mike, would you stay the night? I'd feel better if you
would." She blushed, not wanting him to get the
wrong idea. "You know, just in case Maggie needs
you."

He moved his hand across the table until it covered
one of hers. "I'll stay here as long as you need me."

The feel of his warm hand covering hers immediately conjured up images of the all-too-brief moments they'd shared alone at his place. Her mind's eye
provided instant recall on how he had looked shirtless, with the fire's glow casting golden shadows on his
skin. She could remember in aching detail the way his
naked flesh had felt beneath her hungry fingertips.
Hungry—yes, she was ravenous for him. She hadn't
realized how starved she'd been until he had entered
her life and made her recognize her malnourished
state.

She pulled her hand away as if by breaking their
physical contact she could break the electrical current

that was producing images in her head as efficiently as a film projector.

He didn't seem to notice anything wrong. He reached for another animal cracker. "I think it's about time you teach me sign language. For over a month now, I've been going through strange body contortions and charade games to communicate with Scotty and Jimmy. In the future it would be a lot easier if I knew how to talk to them in their own way."

Molly nodded absently, staring into her coffee cup. In the future... How long a future was he talking about? A day, a month a year? Not fair, Molly old girl, she warned herself. Those kinds of thoughts were not allowed. He'd been very clear in setting the terms of their relationship. No commitments, no strings, and she'd agreed to them. It wasn't fair to wish for more. It wasn't fair for her to wish that he would forget New York and remain in Parsons forever.

"Molly?"

She looked up to find his gaze on her.

"Are you all right?"

She nodded, rubbing a hand across her forehead. "Just a little tired."

"Why don't you go to bed. I'll sit up in case Maggie needs anything."

She hadn't realized she was tired until the words were out of her mouth, but suddenly the thought of bed held enormous appeal. Still, she couldn't just go to sleep and leave him to care for Maggie. The child was her responsibility, as were all the kids, and Molly wasn't accustomed to sharing her responsibilities. "I'll move Maggie into my room to sleep with me and you can bunk on the sofa. I'll wake you up if we need you.'' She didn't give him a chance to protest against the arrangements, but instead got up from the table and moved into the living room where she picked up the still-sleeping Maggie. ''Would you turn down my bed?'' she whispered to him.

He nodded, leading her into the new room, where her furniture had been moved just that morning. When he'd left earlier in the day, the bed had been bare, the top of the dresser empty. It had been as impersonal as a motel room.

Now he was surprised to discover that since then the area had seemed to absorb Molly's essence. The blue floral bedspread was exactly the same shade as her eyes. Her velour robe lay across the overstuffed chair in the corner. The room held her subtle scent. The top of the dresser was covered, not with makeup, not with bottles of perfumes and skin care, but rather with years of children's gifts to her. Clay ashtrays and strange figurines, paper flowers and homemade cards, all proclaimed the room intrinsically Molly's.

He turned down the bedspread and watched in silence as she lay Maggie beneath the sheets. ''I'll get you some blankets from the hall closet.'' She started to walk past him, but he stopped her.

He'd meant to tell her he'd get them, for her to go on to bed and get some rest. But words refused to come to his lips as he pulled her into his arms and embraced her tightly. What he wanted to do was swoop her up in his arms and run away with her. They

wouldn't have to run far—just any place where they
would be alone and could complete what they had begun earlier in the evening. His desire for her had been
growing daily, and now had reached mammoth pro-
portions.

"Are we ever going to get any time alone?" he
growled, pulling her even closer against him.

"I don't know. I hope so." She looked up at him
and her eyes showed him that she was just as disappointed as he was about their interruption.

This knowledge did more to inflame him than anything else she could have said or done. He wanted to
kiss her, invade the sweet warmth of her mouth, move
his hands beneath the jogging suit and feel the silken
softness of her skin. He wanted to move his hips
against hers, show her his growing need, but he didn't.
He gave her a light kiss on the forehead and released
her. Now was not the time to begin something that
couldn't be finished.

"I'll get my sheets and blankets myself. You go on
to bed."

She nodded, overwhelmed by the myriad emotions
he was able to create in her. When he left her room,
she closed the door behind him, changed into her
nightgown and crawled into bed beside Maggie. She
lay on her back aware of the fullness in her breasts, the
aching deep within her that his touch, his kisses had
provoked. He stirred her, creating an empty well, one
she knew only he could fill. She closed her eyes,
imagining what would have happened had she not
made the phone call home earlier in the evening. She

then remembered her fears, her insecurities about Mike. Maybe Maggie's illness had been fate intervening. Maybe it had kept them apart tonight because their love was doomed. She knew now that he had come to Kansas to give himself time to work out where he wanted to go with his professional life. He was here in Parsons on vacation. But what happened to them when the vacation was over?

Mike twisted and turned with a restlessness that had nothing to do with the unfamiliarity of the couch. Molly's sofa was a large overstuffed item that enveloped him with comfort. No, what was causing his restlessness was his mind, which refused to turn off and allow him the peace of unconsciousness.

He heard Maggie begin to cough again, and he waited for Molly to call him. Instead he heard the shower start in the bathroom and knew she was handling the situation herself. He really wasn't surprised. In the past weeks, Molly had shown herself to be extremely capable of handling the children's care. She had never asked him to help her with any of the responsibilities. She didn't need him, he thought, at least not as a helpmate. But he had a feeling she needed him as a man. He had a feeling there were spaces in her soul that only a man could fill, needs that children couldn't satisfy. Molly was an expert at nurturing, but who nurtured Molly? He sighed and turned over, hearing the shower shut off and the house return to silence.

He must have fallen asleep because he awoke some time later to the sound of the shower again. He looked at the illuminated dial of his watch and saw it was almost four o'clock. It hadn't even been midnight when he'd lain down. How many times had Molly been up with Maggie in the intervening hours? She was a strong capable woman, but everyone needed a helping hand once in a while. He rolled off the couch and stood up, surprised at how rested he felt after so few hours of sleep.

He went to the bathroom, knocked briefly on the door, then went inside, his heart expanding at the sight that greeted him. Maggie was asleep in Molly's arms. Molly was asleep, too, her head resting against the glass tub enclosure. Her hair was damp from the steam, waving in a natural curl he'd never noticed before. In sleep, she appeared younger, more vulnerable than he'd ever seen her.

He touched her shoulder, watching as her eyes flew open in surprise. He watched in fascination as the startled expression in her eyes changed, warming and caressing him.

"Let me take her," he said, gesturing to Maggie.

"No, it's all right," she protested, her voice weak with exhaustion.

"Molly, please. I want to help." When she didn't protest further, Mike took the sleeping child from her arms. "You go back to bed. I'm taking her into the living room with me." He left the bathroom and put Maggie down on the sofa. He started to sit down in a chair across the room, but realized he hadn't heard

Molly go to her bedroom. He went back into the bathroom and found her there, her head once again lolled to one side in slumber. Without an ounce of thought, he scooped her up in his arms. Her eyes fluttered briefly, then she placed her arms around his neck and allowed him to carry her into her room.

He placed her on the bed, not surprised when she turned on her side and her breathing resumed the regularity of sleep. He watched her for a long moment, noticing the way her nightgown molded with a lover's closeness to her body. He wanted to crawl into the bed next to her, hold her in his arms, share her body heat. It wasn't passion that made him want to share her bed. It was tenderness, a desire to be next to her while they both slept. It was a strange feeling, this need to connect with her even while she was asleep and unconscious.

He was pulled from his thoughts by the sound of Maggie's stirring in the living room. Reluctantly he covered Molly, gave her a soft kiss on the forehead, then left the room.

Chapter Nine

Molly stirred and stretched languidly, enjoying the warm cocoon her blankets made. The sun shone bright and warm through her window, falling full on her face.

She frowned as wakefulness claimed her. What was the sun doing shining like this so early in the morning? She rolled over and looked at the clock on her bedside stand. Eleven forty-five. Almost noon! Shock jolted her up into a sitting position. She couldn't remember ever sleeping that late. Why was the house so quiet? Had the kids declared mutiny and murdered Mike, or had they given him such a hard time that he had opted to hang them by their thumbs in the barn? This thought caused her to bolt out of bed and run to the living room.

She paused in the doorway, relief surging through her as she gazed at her family. They were all there together. Jimmy and Scotty were sitting on the sofa, and Mike was in the overstuffed chair, Maggie on his lap. Their attention was riveted to the television set, where a VCR had been hooked up and Bambi was meeting Flower the skunk for the very first time. The laughter was harmonious, filling her heart to bursting. She wanted to capture the moment forever in her mind, a memory to be pulled out and treasured at leisure. Her family—how complete it looked with Mike included.

He saw her standing in the doorway, and the smile he gave her, the look in his eyes, spoke of things better left unsaid in front of the children. "Good morning," he finally said.

"Morning," she replied, running a hand self-consciously through her sleep-tousled hair.

"Molly..." Maggie scrambled off Mike's lap and ran to her. "Mike brought us a VCR to use, and he got us some tapes to watch, and I love Bambi. And you slept forever. I wanted to wake you up, but Mike said we had a rough night." The words tumbled over each other in her effort to tell Molly everything.

Molly laughed and swung the little girl up in her arms. "Yes, we did have a rough night. How are you feeling this morning?" She scrutinized Maggie's face, noting that although she was still a little pale, she looked none too worse for the night.

"I feel okay. Mike gave me medicine, and he fixed us all breakfast."

"Oh, he did." Molly looked at him, then at the other kids. "Well, none of you look as if you're suffering ptomaine poisoning, so he must have done all right."

"He made us oatmeal," Maggie stated.

Scotty's fingers flew into the conversation, making Molly laugh.

"What did he say?" Mike asked.

"He said your oatmeal had big lumps the size of my dumplings."

"Lumps?" Mike looked indignant. He jumped up out of his chair and grabbed Scotty by the arm, making the boy's high-pitched giggling fill the room. "I'll give you lumps," Mike exclaimed, tousling the boy's red hair affectionately. He released the boy and grinned at Molly. "If you'll come into the kitchen, I'll pour you a cup of coffee and show you the medicine I got for Maggie."

Molly sat Maggie down on the floor, satisfied that all three kids were absorbed in the movie, then followed him into the kitchen.

"I'm impressed." She smiled at him. "Not only did you feed the kids, you cleaned up the kitchen afterward." She sat down at the table while he poured her a cup of coffee. "How and when did you get the VCR and the medicine?"

"I left Scotty here to keep an eye on Maggie, with strict instructions to wake you up if any problems arose. Then I took Jimmy with me into town, where I picked up the medicine and some VCR tapes. I got the VCR from my house." He set the mug of steaming coffee down in front of her and pulled a chair up next to hers. "I keep telling you I'm a man of many talents. You have yet to discover the area in which I am truly talented," he teased.

"Oh, but I have." She looked at him innocently. "Aren't you talking about your talent as a doctor?"

His eyes were the green of spring foliage, suggesting secret shady places perfect for lovers' trysts. "I'll play the doctor if you'll be my patient." His voice was a soft whisper in her ear.

"But I'm not sick."

"I am." The teasing note was gone from his voice. "I'm sick with wanting you." He moved his fingers up her arm in a slow dance of sensuality that left goose bumps in its wake. "I carried you to bed last night and I wanted more than anything to crawl beneath the covers and make love to you."

"But the children . . ." Molly said, breathless from the pleasurable tingles his fingers were creating in her.

"Yeah, the children," he said dryly. "Always the children." There was no rancor in his voice, only a weary resignation. He removed his fingers from her arm. "Molly, come away with me."

"Can I change my clothes first?" she teased, knowing he was speaking out of sheer frustration.

"I'm serious," he protested, and she could tell by the look in his eyes that he was. Her smile slowly faded.

"Mike, I can't go away with you."

"One night." His eyes burned with hypnotic intensity into hers. "Oh, Molly, don't we owe ourselves one night? We could drive into Kansas City, see a play, go out to eat, then spend the night and come back the next day."

"Oh, Mike...I don't know..." Her heart quickened at the thought of spending a day and night alone with him. It would be a time when she could luxuriate in the role of being a woman who was desired.

"Think about it. We could do it next weekend. We could talk to Leslie about staying with the kids next Saturday, then we could come home on Sunday."

"I'll think about it," she agreed. She wanted to say yes, but a small fear still lurked in the back of her mind. She knew that if she made love with him, her heart would form a commitment that would not be easily ignored. But what of his commitment to her? What would a night of lovemaking mean to him? "I'll think about it," she repeated.

"That's all I'm asking." He stood up. "And now, I think I'll get home. I've left enough Walt Disney tapes in there to keep the kids happy for most of the day. Keep Maggie quiet and you try to rest." He leaned over and kissed her on the forehead. "I'll call later and see if you need anything."

She caught his hand and kissed it, then rubbed it against her cheek. "Mike...I don't know how to thank you for everything you've done."

"You don't need to thank me. I did what I wanted to do." And what he really wanted to do at that moment was take her in his arms and discover exactly how little she was wearing beneath her voluminous nightgown. Instead, he smiled wistfully, then left her sitting at the table.

He was thoughtful as he climbed into his car, surprised at how good he felt. It was the same sort of feeling he used to experience when he'd first begun practicing medicine. It was a rightness in his soul, a sense of accomplishment, that few things had ever brought him. He missed being a doctor. He hadn't realized how much until last night, when his skills as a physician had been needed.

He frowned as he pulled into his driveway and saw an unfamiliar car. A surprised grin quickly usurped his frown as he recognized the man and woman sitting on his front porch.

"Wally, Celia!" Mike bounded out of his car with a renewed burst of energy.

"I told you one of these days I'd surprise you and show up for a visit " Celia said, moving into his arms and offering her cheek for a kiss. "I made Wally come with me because you know how I hate to fly alone."

"Well, I'm glad you did. Wally, it's great to see you again." Mike shook his hand warmly. "How'd you find the place?"

"We flew into Kansas City, then rented the car and followed a map. Once we got into town, we just asked for directions to your place," Wally explained.

"Come in. How long have you been waiting for me?" Mike asked, unlocking the front door and ushering his guests inside.

"Forever!" Celia exclaimed dramatically. "At least it seemed like forever. My God, Mike, how do you stand it out here? It's so quiet and there's nothing to look at."

"You can look at nature at its finest," Mike said in amusement.

"Celia thinks a three-carat diamond is nature at its finest," Wally said dryly, making Mike laugh and Celia flash Wally her infamous drop-dead look.

"Wally's just pouting because I ate his peanuts on the flight," she retorted, perching on the edge of the sofa and looking around with interest. "This isn't too bad, Mike. I half expected you to be living in a log cabin with no running water."

Mike grinned. "We'll see what you think of the plumbing system after you take your first bath here."

As the afternoon wore on and Wally and Celia caught him up on all the gossip and happenings in New York, he realized the distance he'd traveled since leaving the big city could not be measured only in miles. He'd traveled light-years from the life he'd lived there.

It was enjoyable listening to Celia describe the social activities he'd missed, and to Wally tell stories of his plastic-surgery practice.

"Now, tell us what you've been doing with your life for the past month," Celia said, sipping a glass of the wine Mike had decanted moments earlier.

"There really isn't much to tell." He shrugged. "Compared to yours, my life is quite boring."

"What do you do here all day?" Celia asked.

"Actually, for the past couple of weeks I've been helping a neighbor build a room addition."

"Build a room . . ." Celia looked at him in disbelief. "Oh, Mike. It breaks my heart to hear you're actually doing manual labor instead of being the doctor you were born to be."

"What makes you so sure I was born to be a doctor?" Mike said with a laugh.

"Because you look wonderful in a lab coat."

Mike laughed again, then stood up. "What a poor host I am—you guys must be starving. Why don't I whip up some supper?"

"Why don't you take us out on the town? I'll buy supper if you promise me a place where I can get a good steak," Wally suggested.

"Nonsense," Mike returned. "You're my guests, and if we go out, the meal is on me."

Celia also stood up. "Wally, darling, could you fetch our bags from the car? I'd like to freshen up a bit before we go out."

"Sure." Without hesitation, Wally disappeared out the front door to the car.

"Wally's asked me to marry him," Celia said the moment he'd left the house.

"Are congratulations in order?" Mike asked.

"Not yet. I'm not sure I'm going to accept."

"He's a good man. He'd be good for you," Mike observed.

"I suppose." She grinned wickedly. "But have you ever known me to make a decision based on what's good for me?"

They turned as Wally reentered the house, hidden behind a mountain of luggage.

"Here, let me help you." Mike ran to his assistance, grabbing two of the suitcases perched precariously in Wally's arms. "The bedrooms are all upstairs." Mike led the way up the staircase. "Can you manage?" He looked back to see Wally struggling valiantly with the three oversize suitcases he still had.

"I'm fine," Wally huffed. "We're only staying a couple of days, Mike. You'd think Celia could have managed with fewer bags."

Mike chuckled. "Asking Celia to travel light is like asking Santa Claus to utter only one 'ho.'" Mike led him into the larger of the guest bedrooms and set the suitcases down. "Uh, I don't mean to be indelicate, but are you and Celia...uh..."

"No. We're strictly platonic, much to my dismay." Wally grinned. "If you don't have another bedroom, I'll be glad to bunk on the sofa."

"Come on, I'll show you to your room." Mike took Wally down the hall into another room, one with Spartan decor and only a single bed and small dresser. "I've got four bedrooms, but I haven't gotten around to doing much to any of them."

"This is fine," Wally said, placing his single suitcase on the bed.

"If you'll excuse me, I need to take care of a few things before we enjoy a night out on the town." Mike left Wally, then rejoined Celia downstairs. "I put you in the room on the left," he told her. "I need to make a phone call before we leave."

She nodded, still sipping on her glass of wine. "I'm just going to finish this, then I'll run upstairs and freshen up."

Mike left her sitting there and went into the kitchen, where he picked up the phone to call Molly. She'd jumped into his mind off and on during the afternoon, and he was anxious to check and see how she'd gotten along with Maggie.

"Molly," he breathed as she answered the phone.

"Hi, Mike."

He leaned against the kitchen cabinet, basking in the warmth the mere sound of her voice evoked in him. "What are you doing?"

"OD-ing on Walt Disney. I can now sing all the words to all the songs in *Dumbo,* and I'm fast on my way to knowing all the lines of dialogue in *Bambi.*"

"What about Maggie?"

"Oh, she knows all the lines of dialogue in *Bambi.*"

Mike laughed. "That's not exactly what I meant."

"She's fine. A little droopy, and she still has a bit of a cough, but I think the worst is over. What are you doing?"

"I had some friends come in from New York. Remember me telling you about Celia? She's here with her friend, Wally. I was just getting ready to take them out for some dinner. Any chance of your getting away and coming with us?"

"I couldn't, not on such short notice. But you go on and have a good time without me."

"Impossible." He smiled and continued, "Well, I just wanted to warn you in case you heard rumors about my being out on the town with a gorgeous blonde.''

"What makes you think a story like that would bother me?'' Her tone was light and teasing.

"It had better bother you, Molly,'' he growled, then added in a low voice, "Have you thought about what we talked about this morning?''

"A little ''

"And?'' He held his breath, waiting for her answer.

"And I think I need to think about it a little more.'' She laughed as he growled again, this time in frustration.

"I'd better go. I'll call you tomorrow.'' At her murmured goodbye he hung up, a smile lifting the corners of his mouth.

"Who's Molly?''

Mike jumped and turned at the sound of Celia's voice.

"I'd tell you I didn't mean to eavesdrop, but we both know it would be a lie.'' Celia grinned. "So, who's Molly?''

"She's a neighbor. In fact, she's the one I helped build the room addition.''

"Is she also the brood mare you told me about when you first moved in here, the woman with fifteen kids?''

"Actually, three of them are foster kids, and the rest are ones she baby-sits during the days.''

"You've gotten pretty friendly with them?''

Mike nodded.

"Why didn't you invite her and her husband to go out to eat with us this evening? I'd like to meet your new friends."

"There is no husband—Molly isn't married. And I did, but she couldn't get a baby-sitter on such short notice." Mike frowned thoughtfully. "But I could invite her over for dinner tomorrow night." He smiled at Celia. "I'll grill chicken or something. I'd really like for you to meet her. She's a wonderful person."

"I'm looking forward to it," Celia murmured. "Let's just make it real casual, you know—old friends meeting new friends." She smiled at him. "Oh, I'm really looking forward to it." With these words, she turned and left the kitchen, running upstairs to freshen up.

For the second time that evening, Molly hung up after talking to Mike. The second phone call had been an invitation to dinner the following night, a chance to meet his friends from New York. She was both nervous and excited at the prospect, but she shoved these thoughts away. At the moment she had another far greater concern.

Mrs. Bassman, Scotty's social worker, had called earlier in the day to tell Molly that she was bringing his mom out tomorrow and Scotty would be going home. All afternoon, Molly had looked for an opportunity to talk to Scotty about it, but the right time hadn't presented itself. Now she knew it could be put off no longer. The kids had gone to bed only moments be-

fore, and she knew it always took Scotty a while to fall
asleep.

"No time like the present," she murmured getting
up off the sofa and going into the boys' bedroom. She
wasn't surprised to find Jimmy sound asleep and
Scotty lying quietly, his eyes wide open. Molly touched
his shoulder and motioned for him to follow her into
the living room.

"Am I in trouble?" he signed as they sat down on
the sofa.

"Should you be?" Molly returned with a grin.

"I don't think so."

"Mrs. Bassman called today. She has wonderful
news. Your mother is coming to get you tomorrow.
You get to go home."

Scotty looked away, his expression troubled. When
he looked back at Molly he moved his fingers slowly
to ask, "Will I still get to go to school?"

Molly's heart expanded as she saw the worry that
darkened his brown eyes. "Yes, honey. Perhaps not
the same one, but a school like the one you're attend-
ing now." Molly touched his thin freckled arm. "Your
mother understands now how important your school
is. She's anxious to have you home where you belong."

"I'm scared," Scotty signed, and he buried his head
in Molly's shoulder.

She held him close, knowing there was little she
could say that would alleviate his fear. It had been over
a year since he had lived with his mother, and Molly
knew his memories of that time had dimmed and be-

come unfocused. Now he was facing the fear of the unknown. Still, Molly also knew that Mrs. Bassman was a good woman, who would not place Scott back in the care of his mother if she didn't believe all the previous problems had been solved.

Scott sat up. "Can I take my rock collection with me?" he signed.

"Of course," Molly answered, sighing in relief. His question meant he'd accepted the fact that he would be leaving. "You can take everything that belongs to you. Tomorrow you can stay home from school. Mrs. Bassman and your mother won't be here until about noon. That will give us all morning to get you packed up and ready to go."

"Can I go back to bed now?" he asked, as she knew he wanted time alone to sort out his feelings.

She nodded and gave him another hug, then watched as he disappeared into his bedroom. Letting go was so heartrending. As a foster parent, that particular pain came with the territory. She knew that, in her case, loving meant letting go, allowing the kids in her care to leave her behind and get on with their lives. She knew she was merely a resting place, a safe harbor against stormy seas, but when the seas calmed, it was time for each ship to continue its journey.

Is that what I am to Mike, too? A safe harbor, a place to rest until he can continue his journey and resume his life in New York? She'd seen the way his eyes had lit up as he'd dealt with Maggie the other night. She'd seen his efficient professionalism and knew it would be a sin if Mike didn't go back to his medical career. This thought, on the heels of the knowledge of losing Scotty, was simply too painful to deal with.

She pulled herself up off the couch and headed for her bedroom and the oblivion of sleep.

"It looks like that's everything," Molly signed to Scotty, glancing around the bedroom to make sure they hadn't missed packing any items of clothing or treasured objects. "Why don't we go have some lunch?"

Scotty nodded and followed her into the kitchen, Maggie trailing behind, her thumb anchored in her mouth. It had been a traumatic morning when Maggie and Jimmy had learned that Scotty was leaving. Jimmy had taken it particularly hard. Because of their deafness, the two boys had developed a deep bond of friendship. During the emotional goodbye, Mike had called. Molly had spoken with him only a moment, telling him about Scotty's leaving and that she would call him back later in the afternoon.

Scotty had been quiet during the packing process, apparently resigned to the fact he was leaving, but not quite able to hide his anxiety.

They had just sat down to a lunch of peanut-butter-and-jelly sandwiches when a knock had sounded on the door. Scotty stiffened as Molly got up to answer. She was surprised to find Mike on her front porch. "Hi. I didn't expect to see you," she said, opening the door to allow him inside.

"I couldn't let Scotty leave without saying good-bye."

"Where's your company?"

"At my place. I told Wally I had to go out for a while, and Celia was still in bed," he explained. "Where's Scotty?"

"In the kitchen. We were just having lunch." She took his coat and draped it on the sofa.

Scotty's face brightened at the sight of Mike, who joined them for a sandwich.

They had just finished eating when another knock came at the door. This time it was Mrs. Bassman. "Scotty's mother is in the car—I wanted an opportunity to talk to you for a moment first," Mrs. Bassman said after Molly had introduced Mike to the social worker.

"Scotty, would you please take Maggie into the bathroom and wash her sticky face and hands?" Molly signed. The boy nodded and he and Maggie disappeared into the bathroom.

"Molly, I feel really good about this one," Patricia Bassman said when the kids were gone. "Scotty's mother has been going through counseling. She's realized Scotty's deafness is not going to change, that it will have to be dealt with, and she's realized the importance of sending him to a school for the deaf." She broke off as Scotty and Maggie returned to the room. "Scotty, your mother is waiting for you. Are you ready to go?"

"Will you walk me to the car?" Scotty signed to Molly, walking over and grabbing her hand

She patted his hand and nodded, a lump the size of an uncracked walnut lodging in her throat.

"I'll carry out his things," Mike offered, his voice sounding strangely full and unnatural. He put on his coat, then picked up the large box and suitcase that Molly had ready by the front door.

Scotty's mother was sitting in the front seat of Mrs. Bassman's car, but the minute they all stepped out of the house, she got out of the car. In a crowd of a hundred women, Molly would have had little trouble picking out the one who had given birth to Scotty. Her hair was the same copper color as Scotty's, and her thin face was covered with freckles. She looked very young and very nervous as she stood awkwardly next to the car.

When Scotty and Molly got to the bottom of the porch steps, Molly gently extricated her hand from his grasp. She got down on one knee in front of him and signed her goodbye, then stepped back from him. This was always the longest hardest step she ever took, the one that physically removed her from the child's life and sent him on to his new one. She was vaguely aware of Mike's placing the boy's things in the trunk of the car, then rejoining her and Mrs. Bassman. Their attention was riveted to Scotty and the woman who was his mother. "Scotty, I've missed you so much, and I love you." His mother's fingers moved slowly, unaccustomed to the language of the deaf, but her words broke the inertia that claimed Scotty. With a small cry, he ran to his mother and threw his arms around her neck.

"She's been learning sign language in night school," Mrs. Bassman murmured.

"It looks like things are going to be fine now." Molly's voice was low, full of suppressed emotion.

"Well, I guess we'll be on our way. Molly, I'll be in touch."

Molly shook her head, unable to speak. Her emotions were brimming in her throat. Her job was finished now, and Scotty was back where he belonged, but this knowledge made the parting no less painful for her. As the car pulled away, Mike put his arm around Molly's shoulders. She smiled up at him, a trembling smile full of feeling. "You are the most courageous woman I know," Mike said softly.

Molly shook her head. "No, I just know that loss is inevitable in life. You have to have the sunset to appreciate the sunrise. You must have the death of winter to get the splendor of spring."

Mike pulled her close and she stood in his arms, surprised to find that his warm embrace helped to soothe the loss she felt. She burrowed her head in his shoulder, wondering if, when the time came she had to say goodbye to Mike, she would do it with as much dignity as she'd just shown today. Somehow she didn't think so.

Chapter Ten

Mike was in the kitchen with Wally when the doorbell rang. "That must be Molly." He set aside the carrot he'd been peeling for the tossed salad. "I'll be right back." He left the kitchen to answer the door, anxious to see how she had gotten through the remainder of the afternoon. Although she'd held up admirably, he realized how deeply she'd been affected by Scotty's leaving. Mike was going to miss the little scamp, too, who had been able to say more with his facial expressions than most people could say with a hundred words. Scotty had managed to crawl right into Mike's heart, as had all of Molly's kids. Funny, he'd been thinking a lot about what Molly had said earlier that afternoon. Loss was inevitable, and he couldn't insulate himself from it. He'd come out here to escape emotional attachment, but it hadn't worked.

Despite his defenses, Molly and her kids had managed to creep right into the core of his being.

He now opened the door, as always warmed by the sight of her. "Hi."

"Hi." Her smile betrayed a hint of nervous tension.

"Rough afternoon?"

"A little," she admitted. "Oh, this is for dessert." She handed him a plate upon which sat a chocolate bundt cake.

"It looks delicious—and so do you," he added beneath his breath, enjoying the pink blush that tinged her cheeks. She did look delicious, in a blue dress that emphasized her eyes and her peaches-and-cream complexion. "You aren't nervous about meeting Wally and Celia, are you?" he asked, seeing the apprehension in her eyes as she self-consciously ran a hand through her thick hair. "Don't worry, I promise they won't bite." He placed an arm around her and gave her a hug of reassurance. "Come on in and I'll introduce you to Wally. Celia is still upstairs." He led her into the kitchen, where he made the introductions, then went back to his salad making.

As Wally entertained Molly with stories of his plastic-surgery practice, Mike smiled with a feeling of contentment. He'd known Wally would like Molly.

He now looked over to where she was sitting at the table. Her head was thrown back and she was laughing, the sound of which always made the blood pump a little more quickly through his veins. Molly's laugh was infectious . . . beautiful.

"Are you slicing that cucumber or committing it to memory?" Wally asked in amusement, making Mike realize he'd been staring blankly at the green vegetable.

"Is there anything I can do to help?" Molly asked. "I'm not accustomed to just sitting and letting somebody else prepare a meal." She smiled and took a sip of her wine, then added, "But I have to admit, it's definitely something I could get used to."

"You'd better not. The kids would rebel," Mike warned.

"Tell me about these kids," Wally said, and she immediately complied. She felt more relaxed then she had when she'd first arrived. The moment she'd walked up to Mike's door, anxiety had struck her like a boulder hitting her on top of the head. She'd realized how much she wanted to make a good impression on Mike's friends. She was worried that they'd find her small-town, provincial and dull. However, the minute Mike had introduced her to Wally, her fears were allayed. Wally's smile was genuine and his friendly interest in her didn't seem feigned. And of course it helped that Mike's gaze whenever he looked at her was warm and full of silent approval. His eyes told her that it really didn't matter what his friends thought of her, because she pleased him and that was all that mattered.

"Is this some sort of Midwest tradition? That everyone gathers in the kitchen of the house?"

Molly turned at the sound of the low-pitched feminine voice. The woman standing in the doorway, presumably Celia, was Molly's idea of sophistication and glamor. She was wearing a lounging outfit—a tunic top and billowy pants of pale green silk. It was obvious the outfit was a designer original, made to fit her lithe form.

"The kitchen is the heart of a Midwest home," Mike said, opening the oven door to check on his baking chicken.

Wally grinned at Celia. "You may want to look around, familiarize yourself with the way a kitchen looks. You know, just in case you ever feel a desire to do something wild and crazy like cook."

"Heaven forbid, if that ever happens, just put me in a straitjacket and cart me away." She smiled at Molly. "I guess I'll have to introduce myself since the gentlemen seem to have taken leave of their manners. I'm Celia Warren, and you must be Mike's friend, Molly."

Molly had been prepared to dislike Celia. After all, Celia was everything Molly was not—sophisticated, chic, not exactly beautiful, but striking with her boyishly shorn blond hair that emphasized her obscenely high cheekbones and exotic dark eyes.

But as they shared the meal Mike had prepared, she found herself enjoying Celia's droll sense of humor, the arrogance that held a note of self-mockery. Molly had expected a certain amount of condescension, but there was none. In fact, by the time they had finished eating, she realized she and Celia were on the brink of forming a genuine friendship.

Wally and Mike insisted that the two women remain at the table while they cleaned up the dishes. Molly started to protest, but was stopped by Celia, who gave her a look of mock severity. "Don't you dare get up to help. You'll make me look bad, and there's no way I'm going to risk chipping my nail polish for a bunch of dirty dishes."

Molly laughed and held up her hands in surrender. "Sorry, guys. I've been commanded not to help, so it looks like you're on your own."

"That's all right. I got through medical school by working as a busboy, one of the many odd jobs I did to fulfill my desire to become a doctor."

"And Mike worked as a carpenter to get through medical school. Beneath those degrees are just a couple of hardworking stiffs," Molly teased.

"Yes, but Wally *had* to be a working stiff—Mike didn't," Celia said, refilling both her own and Molly's wineglasses. "Mike's father would have bought him Harvard if Mike had expressed an interest."

"I did it my way," Mike said, then snapped his fingers. "Hey, wouldn't that make a catchy line for a song?"

They all groaned.

"Why don't we move into the living room," Mike suggested once the dishes were in the dishwasher.

"Yes, let's," Celia agreed. "Spending too much time in the kitchen always gives me hives." She gestured to the stereo unit as they walked into the living room. "Do you still have that recording of *La Bohème*?"

"Sure, someplace in here." Mike joined her at the stereo and rifled through his record collection as the other two sat on the sofa. "Ah, here it is." He pulled the record from its jacket and placed it on the turntable. Immediately the room filled with the sounds of the New York Philharmonic."

"Oh, Mike, remember the first time we went to see *La Bohème* and I had to explain to you everything that was happening on the stage?" Celia curled up on the chair facing the fireplace where a fire crackled its cheerful tune. "Mike knew nothing about opera until I took him under my wing and broadened his education."

"Yes, but you have to admit, you knew nothing about art until I gave you a few helpful pointers," Mike reminded her with a wry grin.

Molly listened as Celia and Mike began reminiscing, entertaining Wally and her with stories of charity galas, art gallery openings, theater productions, all the many things they had attended together.

It was obvious Mike and Celia shared a past, but Molly was surprised to discover she felt no jealousy. Yes, it was obvious that Mike and Celia had been friends and companions for a long time, but Molly knew with a woman's instincts that they'd never been lovers. There were no unconscious gestures of intimacy between them, no sly glances that spoke of a history of physical closeness.

No, it wasn't Celia that was causing a glimmer of fear to raise its head in Molly's consciousness. As memory recalled memory for the three New Yorkers,

Molly listened with a growing sense of dread. How could Parsons, Kansas, ever compete with the excitement and appeal of New York City? The closest thing Parsons had to an art gallery was Mrs. London's Arts and Crafts store. The only theater production in Parsons was the annual high-school musical, complete with costumes and scenery.

She looked at him now, loving the way his eyes colored with pleasure, the way his dimple appeared and reappeared as elusive as a mirage on a hot summer day. He looked so different from the staid uptight gentleman she'd met almost two months before. Which was the real Mike? Was it the well-bred cosmopolitan man who enjoyed evenings at the symphony and meals at the Plaza? Or was it the man who wrestled with her boys in the middle of the living-room floor and relished chicken and dumplings, and pies made from scratch?

"Molly, would you like some more wine?" Mike smiled at her from across the room.

"Oh, no, thank you," she demurred. "I think I've already had one glass too many."

"How about a cup of coffee?"

"That sounds good."

"I could use a cup, too," Wally said.

"Need any help?" Molly asked, more from habit than anything else.

"As a matter of fact, yes." Mike's grin was wicked, speaking of intimacies yet to be enjoyed.

Molly blushed as she got up and followed him into the kitchen. He caught her up in his arms the moment she walked through the doorway. His arms were tight around her and his lips moved softly against her temple. "Hmm, I've wanted to do this all evening," he murmured.

She clung to him, finding his warm closeness a welcome respite against the confusing uncertainty she'd been feeling. The different worlds she and Mike were from had never been more apparent than this evening with his friends. But standing in his embrace, held in the shelter of his arms, her uncertainty ebbed away.

His lips met hers in a soft kiss. "Molly, I—"

"Hmm, looks like something is brewing in here besides coffee." Celia walked into the kitchen, casting them both a sly smile. Molly quickly moved out of Mike's arms.

"Oh, don't let me stop you. I was just going to get myself some more wine," Celia said, but the moment was lost, and Mike moved to the cabinet to get out the coffee.

Minutes later they were all back in the living room, Wally, Mike and Molly enjoying a cup of freshly brewed coffee and Celia sticking stubbornly to the wine.

"I have an announcement to make." Mike cleared his throat and stood up. He looked at them all, his gaze lingering on Molly. They watched him curiously.

He was like a little boy who couldn't wait to share a secret, Molly thought, enjoying the way his eyes danced, the way his face reflected his need to share something important with them.

"I came to Parsons a couple months ago needing to deal with a personal crisis of sorts, wanting to discover exactly what I was going to do with my career as a doctor." His gaze was warm on Molly. "It took a very special woman to teach me about courage, about loss...and about rewards." He paused dramatically. "I've decided to return immediately to medicine."

Wally and Celia went into effusive cheers, congratulating him on his decision. "I knew this farmer-in-the-dell stuff wouldn't last," Celia exclaimed smugly.

Molly knew she was smiling, she could feel her mouth curve upward in the appropriate facial expression, but she felt as if her body had been slammed by the biggest, most vicious tackler from the Kansas City Chiefs football team.

"Will your landlord here let you out of your lease?" Wally asked.

"If he doesn't you can just buy your way out of it," Celia said airily. "It's a good thing Wally and I are here—we can help you pack."

"Whoa!" Mike laughed, raising his hands to still his friends. "You two are moving way too fast. I haven't decided that far ahead. I've just decided to go back to doctoring, but I'm not sure where."

"But of course you'll go back to New York." They were the most difficult words Molly had ever spoken, but she felt they were necessary. Right. "New York is your home. It's where you have an established practice."

Mike's smile wavered slightly. "Well, sure, but that doesn't mean I have to go back there."

"Of course you'll go back to New York." Molly smiled at him, her insides churning. She wanted to yell, scream at him not to go. But, she had no more right to keep him with her than she'd ever had with any of her foster children. She was accustomed to being a temporary sort of thing. What she hadn't counted on was falling helplessly in love with Mike Wakefield.

She was grateful when the conversation turned to a general discussion of burnout. She listened to the talk swirling around her, trying to make sense of her conflicting emotions about Mike. It was nearing ten o'clock when she decided it was time to leave. She needed to be by herself and sort out the confusing emotions battling in her brain, tearing out her heart.

"I need to get back home," she said, rising from the couch.

"But it's only ten o'clock. The night is only just beginning," Celia protested.

"Out here in the country, where people rise before dawn, the night is nearly half-gone." Molly smiled. "Besides, I promised the baby-sitter I'd be home early."

"I'll walk you out," Mike said after Molly had said her goodbyes to Wally and Celia.

"They like you," Mike said as they walked out into the cold night air.

"I like them, too."

He threw his arm around her shoulder as they walked toward the station wagon. "So, are you going to be able to get away and spend the weekend with me?''

''Mike, I really don't think the timing is right just now. With Scotty gone, I don't want to leave the other kids right now.'' The lie came easily to her lips. There was no way she was going to go away with him, make love to him, knowing it was just a matter of time before he left Parsons behind. She'd been a foster parent for years, and she'd long ago learned to cope with the wrench of losing the children who passed through her life. What she hadn't been prepared for, what she felt so ill-equipped to handle, was the prospect of Mike passing out of her life.

''I've got to go,'' she said, using every ounce of her self-control to hold back the tears that threatened.

She started to turn away and get into the car, but he stopped her, whirling her around, a smile on his face. ''You don't really think I'm going to let you leave without giving you a proper good-night kiss.''

She wanted to protest, didn't want the further complication to her emotions that his kiss, his touch, always evoked. But as his lips moved to hers, she found herself drinking of him, returning his kiss with all the longing, all the love, she had in her heart.

''Molly, I could stay here in Parsons, start a new practice,'' he said as he broke the kiss.

''That's the most ridiculous thing I've ever heard.'' Molly forced a light laugh. ''You don't belong here.''

Mike wasn't sure exactly what he'd been expecting, but he was surprised by the wave of disappointment that surged through him. Maybe she was right. He suddenly realized that the kiss she'd just given him hadn't been a good-night kiss. It had been a kiss of goodbye.

"Good night, Mike." She moved out of the warmth of his arms and into the cold interior of her car. It wasn't until she'd driven out of his driveway that she allowed her tears to fall.

Chapter Eleven

"Damn," Molly muttered beneath her breath when she sloshed coffee over the rim of her mug, staining the pristine tablecloth she'd just placed on the kitchen table. She moved the mug and yanked the tablecloth off, bundling it into a ball and throwing it on the floor. It was the last straw. Tears spurted to her eyes, as unwelcome as ants at a picnic. She swiped at them angrily and flopped down in a kitchen chair. Thank God none of the children were around to see what a basket case she was. Leslie had arrived earlier, insisting that she felt like spending the day in the pleasurable company of a little girl.

Molly hadn't protested as Leslie rounded up Maggie and took off, promising to have her back by the time the others got home from school.

Molly had spent a miserable night huddled under her electric blanket, wondering if it was possible to be shocked to death by lying beneath the electrical device and crying a river of tears. She'd hoped her tears would be cathartic, that she would awaken in the morning feeling cleansed and in control. She'd hoped that when she got out of bed, she could leave her pain and sense of loss behind, along with her tearstained pillow. But it hadn't been so. When she'd opened her eyes, her very first thought had been that soon Mike would be out of her life forever, and with this thought came a ripping tormenting emptiness. Why was it that she hadn't realized she was in love with him until last night, when he'd announced his decision to return to medicine, and she'd been faced with the fact that he would be returning to New York.

She's been a fool to allow him to become a part of her life, a part of her family. He's warned her from the very beginning that his life here was only temporary. But even though she had agreed to his terms, heard his words of caution, her heart had been deaf to his warning.

"Buck up, old girl," she now said aloud, sniffling indelicately. She'd spent a lifetime being strong enough to say goodbye to loved ones. She wasn't about to allow this one to get her down. "With or without Mike Wakefield, life goes on and I have a family depending on me." She jumped as a knock sounded on the front door.

"Mrs. Bassman, please come in." Molly greeted the social worker in surprise and led her into the living room. "There isn't any problem with Scotty, is there?" she asked worriedly.

"Oh, no, nothing like that. In fact, I've come about Maggie. I have some wonderful news." She looked around as if to make sure the little girl wasn't nearby.

"Don't worry, Maggie went to a friend's house for the day," Molly assured her.

"Well, I have the nicest news!" Mrs. Bassman exclaimed. "Maggie is now officially adoptable and we're going to be actively seeking to place her permanently."

"Oh, that's wonderful." Molly forced a smile, digging her fingernails into the palms of her hands.

"I know you like to keep abreast on what's happening to each child. And you always do such a wonderful job preparing the children for their new lives. I suggest you start with Maggie right away. It won't take long to place somebody as lively and loving as little Maggie."

Molly nodded.

"Now, I really must run. You know us social workers—underpaid and overworked." Mrs. Bassman rose. "I'll be in touch," she said, as Molly saw her out.

Once she was gone, Molly sagged down on the sofa, grief swiftly overtaking her. Not my Magpie, she thought, trying to imagine life without her little ray of sunshine. Where would social services place her? Would they give her parents who would understand

her night terrors? People who would fill her need to be
held in the darkness? Oh God, it was all too much.
First Mike, and now Maggie. Mrs. Bassman had said
she was good at preparing the children for new lives,
but who prepared Molly?

Still, as soon as Maggie returned home that afternoon, Molly decided to talk to her. She knew if she put
it off, it would never get done.

"We need to talk," she said, pulling Maggie onto
her lap. "Remember how we've talked before about
how this is a place you only stay for a little while, just
until Mrs. Bassman can find you a real mommy and
daddy?"

Maggie nodded and stuck her thumb in her mouth,
eyeing Molly solemnly.

"Well, Mrs. Bassman stopped by today and she had
wonderful news. You're adoptable and they're going
to start looking for a real family for you."

"I don't want a real mommy and daddy. I just want
to stay here with you." Maggie wound her arms
around Molly's neck.

"Oh, honey, you can't stay here forever. Someplace out there are a man and a woman who can't wait
to have a little girl just like you."

"Don't you love me anymore?"

Molly's heart was breaking, shattering into a thousand pieces that she knew she could never quite put
back together. "Of course I still love you. I'll always
love you."

Maggie was too young to understand that because Molly loved her so very much she had to let her go. Molly wanted to see Maggie in a real family, with the security and love that two parents could offer. The same way she loved Mike, and therefore had to let him go back to the life that really made him happy.

She pulled Maggie away from her and looked into the little girl's overbright blue eyes. "I'll always love you, my little bean, but I want you to have a real family. A mommy and daddy who will tuck you in each night and give you kisses that make you feel happy right down to your toes. Now, how about a little nap for you?"

So, this is how it feels when your life is falling apart, Molly thought moments later when Maggie was tucked in for a nap. She'd thought the pain of losing Mike would ebb, but losing Maggie and Mike in one fell swoop was almost too much to bear.

Mike will go back to New York and get on with his life, and Maggie will be placed in a loving family. And me, somehow I'll survive, she thought, hearing the sound of the kids arriving home from school.

"Where's Maggie?" Carrie asked as she entered the house. "I made her a paper flower today in art class." Carrie was always making little knickknacks for Maggie.

"She's in the bedroom," Molly answered.

Carrie disappeared down the hallway. She came back out moments later, a curious expression on her face. "She's not there. The window's open and her overnight bag is gone. It looks like she's run away."

"Whoa, what's all this?" Mike said with surprise, entering his kitchen to find Celia with her bags all packed.

"Wally and I are leaving this evening," Celia answered.

"So soon?" Mike poured himself a cup of coffee and joined her at the table.

"Wally's got to get back to his practice." She smiled. "If he's going to keep his wife in the manner in which she is accustomed, he's going to have to maintain a thriving business."

"So, you've decided to marry him." Mike nodded his approval. Wally would make Celia happy. He was indulgent, but not weak. He adored her, but he wasn't blind to her faults.

Celia leaned forward over the table, her eyes lacking their customary humor and naughtiness. "I couldn't agree to marry Wally until I came out here and saw you."

"Me?" Mike looked at her in surprise. "What could I possibly have to do with your decision to marry Wally?"

"Oh, Mike, you are quite an intelligent man, but you've always been rather dense when it comes to members of the opposite sex." The wicked little sparkle was back in her eyes. "Before I accepted Wally's proposal, I needed to come out here and make sure that you weren't coming back to New York. You see, I had this fantasy that you and I..." She let her voice trail off as Mike's eyes widened in shock.

"Celia, I never knew... I mean, I didn't think..."

"Oh, stop stuttering and don't worry. My heart isn't broken. In fact, my heart was never really involved," she confessed. "I just thought we'd make a fantastic-looking couple—you so tall, dark and handsome, and me, thin, blond and beautiful. I also thought it would be a smart business move—your skills as a doctor and my social connections."

Mike smiled despite his surprise, amused by the reasons she'd chosen him as a prospective husband. "I hope your reasons for deciding to marry Wally are a little more profound."

"Oh, they are. Although I have to admit, Wally doesn't look nearly as good in a tuxedo as you do and he certainly can't dance as well." She looked down into her coffee cup for a moment, and when she looked back up, he was surprised to see her face was naked, devoid of the social pretenses she wore like a shield. "Wally loves me. He knows I'm vain and self-ish. He knows I'm spoiled and a horrid snob, and he still loves me. And I love him for that." She smiled again, the smile of a woman sure of herself and her direction in life. "Besides, I really can't see myself as the wife of a country doctor."

Mike looked at her in surprise. "What makes you think I'm going to be a country doctor?"

Celia shrugged. "It's obvious you're happy here."

He nodded. "I am happy here, happier than I've ever been in my entire life." He smiled reflectively. "I'm not sure exactly what I was looking for when I decided to come out here for a year, but I think I've found it."

"And I have a feeling much of your happiness here revolves around Mother Goose next door."

Mike laughed at her description, then sobered. "Yes, Molly and the kids have become an integral part of my happiness." He frowned. "I thought she felt the same way, but now I don't know what to think."

"What do you mean?"

Mike shrugged. "If she wanted me to stay here and be a part of her life, then why did she tell me to go back to New York? Why didn't she ask me to stay here?" He was aware of the starkness of emotion in his voice.

"Mike." Celia placed a hand on his arm. "Molly is one of those women I've never been able to understand, a totally selfless woman who wants only the happiness of those she loves. She thinks you would be happiest in New York, and so that's where she wants you to be, regardless of her own personal feelings. And she loves you."

"How do you know that?"

Celia smiled. "It's so obvious. It's in her eyes when she looks at you, in her smile when she smiles at you. All you have to do is convince her that your happiness lies here, with her." Celia patted his arm. "Now, when should we plan a return trip out here for the wedding?''

Marry Molly? The moment Wally and Celia left, the words flashed through his head, and the moment he contemplated the prospect, he knew the rightness of it. He'd been so busy enjoying every moment spent with her, so involved in the daily joy of loving her, he hadn't thought about the future. But now the prospect loomed before him. Like a rainbow promising sunny days, like Cupid promising love, the prospect of marriage to Molly promised days of sunshine and laughter, years of love forever after. Molly and her kids had helped him heal, but that wasn't enough. He wanted to spend the rest of his life with them. He ran to the kitchen cabinet and grabbed his car keys.

What if Celia was wrong? What if Molly didn't love him? He refused to consider it, finding the thought too painful to contemplate.

He hurried to the front door, needing to get to Molly as soon as possible, tell her that she was stuck with him forever. He threw open the front door and jumped, surprised to see Maggie standing there, a small suitcase in her hand. ''Well, well, what have we here?''

''I runned away,'' Maggie announced, walking inside and putting her suitcase down on the sofa.

''Hmm, that's pretty serious. Why'd you run away?'' Mike sat down and was immediately joined by Maggie.

"I'm 'doptable, and I don't wanna be. Molly says Mrs. Bassman is going to find me a new mommy and daddy, but I don't want them."

Mike's heart instantly ached, knowing the hurt Molly must be feeling. He was surprised at how deeply the thought of losing little Maggie affected him, too. He also knew that Molly was probably frantic with worry over Maggie's disappearance.

"I don't need new parents," Maggie continued. "I like the ones I have just fine."

"What ones do you have?" Mike asked.

"You and Molly, silly grouch." Maggie looked at him as if his question was incredibly stupid.

Mike thought about her words, realizing the trust that Maggie had placed in him. She thought of him and Molly as her parents, her family. She'd known, in her childish innocence, the depth of Mike and Molly's feelings for one another. *Surely Maggie and I can't both be wrong,* Mike thought.

"You know what I think, Magpie? I think it's time we had a little talk with Molly, straighten out a few things." He stood up and held out his hand to the little girl.

Maggie eyed him warily. "Are you gonna make it so I'm not 'doptable?"

"I'm going to do my best," Mike promised, smiling as Maggie got up off the couch and grabbed his hand.

It took them only minutes to get to Molly's, and as soon as they drove into the driveway, Molly ran out of the house and right into Mike's arms. "Oh, Mike, Maggie's gone," she gasped, tears skittering like silver raindrops down her cheeks.

"No, I'm not," Maggie called, getting out of the car.

"Oh, Maggie!" Molly released Mike and caught the little girl up in her arms, burying her face in the sunshine scent of her hair. "Don't you ever do anything like this again," she said, not knowing whether to spank her or hug her. She settled for an extra-tight hug.

"I won't, because Mike is going to fix everything. He's going to make me so I'm not 'doptable.'"

Molly set Maggie down on the ground. "Why don't you go inside. The others will be glad to see you safe and sound. You tell them I said everyone can have cookies and milk." Molly's voice was deceptively calm as she looked at Mike, her eyes filled with anger.

"Okay," Maggie agreed, skipping toward the house.

"How dare you!" Molly said. "How dare you tell her that you're going to fix everything. You have no right to interfere."

"But I *am* going to try to fix everything. Don't you think the adoption board would allow a country doctor and his wife to adopt Maggie?"

"A country...wife..." Molly's anger seeped away like water on sun-parched soil. "What are you talking about?"

"I'm talking about us. You and me getting married and adopting Maggie." He moved closer to her, his nearness making Molly ache with need, with want. "Molly, I'm talking about us spending the rest of our lives together, raising these kids, and maybe a few of our own." He put his hands on her shoulders and pulled her toward him.

"No, you're talking nonsense," Molly protested, trying to struggle out of his arms, but he held her steadfast. She gave up her struggling, weak with grief. "Mike, please." The words were uttered in a hoarse whisper. "Please let me go. You're only making it hurt more...."

"Molly, I don't understand. Why should it hurt you that we love each other?"

She looked up at him, her eyes full of pain. "Because if you stay here, you'll eventually come to resent me for keeping you here. You'll miss New York and you'll grow to hate me, and I couldn't stand that." She tore her gaze away from him. "I saw the way you looked when you were talking with Wally and Celia. Your eyes lit with pleasure as you talked about your experiences in New York. I... I can't compete with that."

"You don't have to." He placed his hand beneath her chin and raised her head so that she was looking at him once again. "Molly, what you saw in my eyes last night was the pleasure of memories, and happiness in knowing that particular life was behind me. You saw a man who was at peace with the past, but looking forward to a future here with you. The only art I'm interested in is refrigerator art. The only excitement I want is the kind that comes with whooping cough, and fish hooks through fingers, and making love to the woman I love." He brushed a strand of hair away from her face. "The only thing I need in this life is to wake up beside you every morning, hold you in my arms at night, know you'll be there to love and support me when I have a professional loss or setback. Molly, I don't want New York. I want you."

Molly looked up at him, loving him and, more importantly, believing what he was saying. She remembered the unhappy tense man she had first met. He was not the same man she now held in her arms. This man was happy here, and what they felt for each other was real and wonderful, and forever. "Did you really mean what you said—about the country doctor and his wife?" she asked.

"I'd planned to do this under more romantic conditions, but..." He pulled away from her and went down on one knee. "Molly Smith, would you do me the honor of becoming my wife?"

"Yes," she answered breathlessly, laughing as he stood up and reached for her once again, this time to give her a kiss that stole her breath and made her tingle from head to toe.

The kiss was broken by the sound of cheering. They turned to see all the kids standing on the front porch, clapping and hooting with excitement.

"Just one thing," Mike murmured against her ear. "You have to promise me that somehow, someway, we'll get a chance to be alone and consummate this marriage."

Molly smiled, wrapping her arms around him once again. "That, my darling, is a promise I'll keep over and over again." And with the children still cheering, Molly and Mike kissed again, a kiss that held the promise of a lifetime of love.

* * * * *

Silhouette ❦ Romance®

COMING NEXT MONTH

AVAILABLE THIS MONTH:

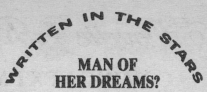

MAN OF HER DREAMS?

Will sexy Libra Jared Dalton make Kendall Arden's dreams come true? Find out in Patricia Ellis's PILLOW TALK, October's WRITTEN IN THE STARS book!

Kendall didn't know what she was letting herself in for when she agreed to help the perfect Libra with his psychology project. Jared's every glance awoke feelings she'd never before experienced—and promised to fulfill *all* her fantasies....

PILLOW TALK by Patricia Ellis ... only from Silhouette Romance in October. It's WRITTEN IN THE STARS!

EVAN
Diana Palmer

Diana Palmer's bestselling LONG, TALL TEXANS series
continues with EVAN....

Anna Cochran is nineteen, blond and beautiful—and she wants
Evan Tremayne. Her avid pursuit of the stubborn, powerfully
built rancher had been a source of amusement in Jacobsville,
Texas, for years. But no more. Because Evan Tremayne is about
to turn the tables...and pursue her!

Don't miss EVAN by Diana Palmer, the eighth book in her
LONG, TALL TEXANS series. Coming in September...only
from Silhouette Romance.

SILHOUETTE®
OFFICIAL SWEEPSTAKES
RULES

NO PURCHASE NECESSARY

1. To enter, complete an Official Entry Form or 3"× 5" index card by hand-printing, in plain block letters, your complete name, address, phone number and age, and mailing it to: Silhouette Fashion A Whole New You Sweepstakes, P.O. Box 9056, Buffalo, NY 14269-9056.

   No responsibility is assumed for lost, late or misdirected mail. Entries must be sent separately with first class postage affixed, and be received no later than December 31, 1991 for eligibility.

2. Winners will be selected by D.L. Blair, Inc., an independent judging organization whose decisions are final, in random drawings to be held on January 30, 1992 in Blair, NE at 10:00 a.m. from among all eligible entries received.

3. The prizes to be awarded and their approximate retail values are as follows: Grand Prize — A brand-new Ford Explorer 4×4 plus a trip for two (2) to Hawaii, including round-trip air transportation, six (6) nights hotel accommodation, a $1,400 meal/spending money stipend and $2,000 cash toward a new fashion wardrobe (approximate value: $28,000) or $15,000 cash; two (2) Second Prizes — A trip to Hawaii, including round-trip air transportation, six (6) nights hotel accommodation, a $1,400 meal/spending money stipend and $2,000 cash toward a new fashion wardrobe (approximate value: $11,000) or $5,000 cash; three (3) Third Prizes — $2,000 cash toward a new fashion wardrobe. All prizes are valued in U.S. currency. Travel award air transportation is from the commercial airport nearest winner's home. Travel is subject to space and accommodation availability, and must be completed by June 30, 1993. Sweepstakes offer is open to residents of the U.S. and Canada who are 21 years of age or older as of December 31, 1991, except residents of Puerto Rico, employees and immediate family members of Torstar Corp., its affiliates, subsidiaries, and all agencies, entities and persons connected with the use, marketing, or conduct of this sweepstakes. All federal, state, provincial, municipal and local laws apply. Offer void wherever prohibited by law. Taxes and/or duties, applicable registration and licensing fees, are the sole responsibility of the winners. Any litigation within the province of Quebec respecting the conduct and awarding of a prize may be submitted to the Régie des loteries et courses du Québec. All prizes will be awarded; winners will be notified by mail. No substitution of prizes is permitted.

4. Potential winners must sign and return any required Affidavit of Eligibility/Release of Liability within 30 days of notification. In the event of noncompliance within this time period, the prize may be awarded to an alternate winner. Any prize or prize notification returned as undeliverable may result in the awarding of that prize to an alternate winner. By acceptance of their prize, winners consent to use of their names, photographs or their likenesses for purposes of advertising, trade and promotion on behalf of Torstar Corp. without further compensation. Canadian winners must correctly answer a time-limited arithmetical question in order to be awarded a prize.

5. For a list of winners (available after 3/31/92), send a separate stamped, self-addressed envelope to: Silhouette Fashion A Whole New You Sweepstakes, P.O. Box 4665, Blair, NE 68009.

PREMIUM OFFER TERMS

To receive your gift, complete the Offer Certificate according to directions. Be certain to enclose the required number of "Fashion A Whole New You" proofs of product purchase (which are found on the last page of every specially marked "Fashion A Whole New You" Silhouette or Harlequin romance novel). Requests must be received no later than December 31, 1991. Limit: four (4) gifts per name, family, group, organization or address. Items depicted are for illustrative purposes only and may not be exactly as shown. Please allow 6 to 8 weeks for receipt of order. Offer good while quantities of gifts last. In the event an ordered gift is no longer available, you will receive a free, previously unpublished Silhouette or Harlequin book for every proof of purchase you have submitted with your request, plus a refund of the postage and handling charge you have included. Offer good in the U.S. and Canada only.

SLFW - SWPR

SILHOUETTE® OFFICIAL SWEEPSTAKES ENTRY FORM

4-FWSRS-2

Complete and return this Entry Form immediately – the more entries you submit, the better your chances of winning!

- Entries must be received by **December 31, 1991.**
- A Random draw will take place on **January 30, 1992.**
- No purchase necessary.

Yes, I want to win a FASHION A WHOLE NEW YOU Sensuous and Adventurous prize from Silhouette:

Name _____ Telephone _____ Age _____

Address _____

City _____ State _____ Zip _____

Return Entries to: Silhouette **FASHION A WHOLE NEW YOU,**
P.O. Box 9056, Buffalo, NY 14269-9056   © 1991 Harlequin Enterprises Limited

PREMIUM OFFER

To receive your free gift, send us the required number of proofs-of-purchase from any specially marked FASHION A WHOLE NEW YOU Silhouette or Harlequin Book with the Offer Certificate properly completed, plus a check or money order (do not send cash) to cover postage and handling payable to Silhouette FASHION A WHOLE NEW YOU Offer. We will send you the specified gift.

- -

OFFER CERTIFICATE

Item	A. SENSUAL DESIGNER VANITY BOX COLLECTION (set of 4) (Suggested Retail Price $60.00)	B. ADVENTUROUS TRAVEL COSMETIC CASE SET (set of 3) (Suggested Retail Price $25.00)
# of proofs-of-purchase	18	12
Postage and Handling	$3.50	$2.95
Check one	☐	☐

Name _____

Address _____

City _____ State _____ Zip _____

Mail this certificate, designated number of proofs-of-purchase and check or money order for postage and handling to: Silhouette **FASHION A WHOLE NEW YOU** Gift Offer, P.O. Box 9057, Buffalo, NY 14269-9057. Requests must be received by December 31, 1991.

ONE PROOF-OF-PURCHASE

4-FWSRP-2

To collect your fabulous free gift you must include the necessary number of proofs-of-purchase with a properly completed Offer Certificate.

© 1991 Harlequin Enterprises Limited

See previous page for details.